THE PRINCESS OF FIRE

The Firelight Series

MATY EITNER

The Princess of Fire

Copyright © 2024 by Maty Eitner.

MILTON & HUGO L.L.C.
4407 Park Ave., Suite 5
Union City, NJ 07087, USA

Website: *www. miltonandhugo.com*
Hotline: *1- 888-778-0033*
Email: *info@miltonandhugo.com*

Ordering Information:
Quantity sales. Special discounts are granted to corporations, associations, and other organizations. For more information on these discounts, please reach out to the publisher using the contact information provided above.

Library of Congress Control Number: 2024920139
ISBN-13:   979-8-89285-327-9   [Paperback Edition]
                  979-8-89285-328-6   [Digital Edition]

Rev. date: 11/06/2024

This book is dedicated to all my fellow firefighters, the Lieutenant, and the division chief who taught me to control my fires.

I also thank my parents and friends for supporting my career choice.

WARNING

This book has trigger warnings, including Murder, assault, stalking, blood and gore, cursing, kinks, and explicit sexual scenes, consensual and Non-consensual.

PROLOGUE

I had just fallen asleep when the tones sounded. "Structure fire at Hope Manufacturing, " the voice over the speakers said. Driving the battalion truck to the scene, I couldn't help but think about my family: Dylan on his honeymoon, Tyler about to have his first date with a girl he has liked for almost a year, Codi about to graduate high school and go on to college to get her EMT certification—my little mini-me.

Her mother is upset about it, but I assure her there is nothing to be worried about. Her boyfriend is hesitant to say anything about it.

I arrive at the scene, smoke pluming from every opening and flames shooting up the industrial building. As I get out, Young Fitz jogs to my side, eager to begin his training to become cheif.

"We have four units on defense. Neighboring cities are on their way to help."

Perfect.

"Is everyone evacuated?" I ask, shouting over the chatter of the radio.

"Yes, sir. As far as I'm aware."

"Good. Let's get the workers behind the trucks where it's safer and have medics check them out." I noticed the hazardous chemicals sign on the side of the building. "What chemicals are in there?"

"I'm not sure, personally. I know large amounts of acetone, oxygen tanks, and propane tanks off the delta side of the building."

"Get crews protecting those propane tanks before they ignite."

"Copy!" Fitz says, running to make commands.

I command multiple crews on their defense when a worker grabs my shoulder.

"Sir, we're missing someone. Martenez is still inside. He works upstairs." The worker shouts.

Fuck...

Just then, a voice calls out from an upstairs window. I frantically look around to find a crew available for a search and rescue just as a small explosion comes from the bottom floor. The flames are too much for the crews, but I'm not letting that guy burn.

"Head back with the other workers. I'll take care of this."

The man nods and retreats behind the engine. I quickly run to the rescue, grab a spare SCBA, turn on the tank, strap a mask to it, and run into the building.

A few firefighters tried to stop me but needed to be faster.

Not long after I made it inside, the engines' horns sounded three times, alerting everyone to evacuate.

Before I could think, a wall of flames charged at me, and then...

AN EXPLOSION.

CHAPTER

1

How I made it through the academy is beyond me. I'm small, fragile, and barely strong enough to carry the smallest hose in the department dry. Even my turnout bag is a struggle. My turnouts had to be custom-made to fit my small stature. But somehow, I made it to graduation. I am standing in front of the crowd with my uniform on. The shortest one in the class. I wish my dad were here to see this—his youngest child following in his footsteps. I doubt I'll make chief someday. Hell, I'll barely make it as a basic firefighter. But at least I'm trying.

I wish my mom were here, too. She refuses to support my career after what happened to Dad. "I will not bury another person in this family while I'm alive," she would always say. Her head about exploded when I told her I got accepted into the academy. My brothers went on to be family men, working regular blue-collar jobs to support their families. Big houses, beautiful wives, nice cars, laughing kids, everything the average person wants. But me? I like adventure and risk, and I do not care if I die as long as I'm helping someone. I want to be like my dad. Brave, strong. Too bad I'm built like my mother.

"Congratulations to the graduating class!" Chief Fitz announces.

The crowd claps, and the guys beside me stand tall. They are towering even more over me. Chief Fitz reads off names one by one, declaring them firefighters of Clearwater. A city named for the once clear lakes surrounding it, now either dried up or polluted to the point of no visibility.

"Congratulations, firefighter Dovetch."

I snap to attention when hearing my sir's name. The name of my father. The name I will hold on to forever. Chief Fitz brings my badge to me and pins it on my left side. I made it. In some magical way, I made it. The graduation ceremony was long, swearing us all in as firefighters. Once the ceremony is done, there's the party after. That was my queue to leave. My body is still sore from the CPAT test I struggled through. I go home to run a hot bath to soothe my aching muscles.

I light some candles to illuminate my tiny one-bedroom apartment. The floor-to-ceiling window of the living room makes the apartment look much nicer than it is. But, some skilled decorating has helped to make this tiny place home. Rain speckles the large windows and floods the streets below. The traffic lights reflected off every puddle. Sometimes, I sit on the couch and stare out the window for hours, watching the city life go on. Drunk girls stumbling down the road calling for a cab, the homeless guy outside the convenience store begging for spare change, the guy who decided to park in front of the fire hydrant getting his car towed.

My short, dark brown hair is still damp from the cold rain I had to walk through to get home, plastered to my forehead. I cut my hair short the day before the academy. It would be much more manageable when in a rush during a call and with how much I sweat fully geared up. It would be just one less thing I have to worry about.

The bath water is hot, but it tames my sore muscles, stinging slightly as I fully immerse myself in the minty Epson salts sprinkled in. I'm small enough to be fully submerged in the water. Even my breasts relax just under the surface. The sound of the rain pattering on the living room windows adds extra relaxation. It's my last free night before going on my first shift, so I'm taking advantage of the freedom. A cold beer, a hot bath, peaceful sounds. It's still not immensely calming the nerves building in my gut. Maybe I should have gotten a regular day job like Mom wanted. But that doesn't feel like my nature. It's not in my blood. Dylan and Tyler never even considered going into fire service after Dad. They listened to Mom and stayed safe.

I look over to my turnouts bag, lying by the front door, packed and ready for service. The 'firefighter' and 'fire rescue' patches are perfectly placed on the sides. I thought for sure I would be excited by now. I slide down, submerging my head under the water. The world drifts away under the warmth.

The walk to the station didn't take as long as I thought. The rain stopped just enough for me to make it twenty minutes early to my shift. The ladder truck and engine are resting in their bays, shiny and clean, standing proud in their assigned spots.

"Are you Dovetch?" A deep voice from my right catches my attention.

"Yes, sir, I am," I answer politely.

"I am Captain Kelso. Welcome to station 31."

He holds his hand out, and I take it in mine and give a firm handshake. At least as firm as my tiny hands can provide.

"We are about to sit down for breakfast if you want to join us. There's fresh coffee as well. You'll need all the caffeine you can get."

He wasn't wrong. The academy was rough enough. A 24-hour shift would require a lot to keep me awake and focused. However, adrenaline alone will help that department if we get a fire call. Walking into the firehouse was like walking into a new school. Everything smelled different. There were new faces, and I was nervous. The kitchen was huge. Four fridges, two sinks, two coffee makers, two stoves, multiple cabinets lining the walls, granite countertops, and grey stone backsplashes. All the appliances were stainless steel, with no streaks on them. Not even a single crumb on the counters or a dish in the sink. The place sparkled. To my right, a long, wooden dining table is covered in a food buffet: eggs, bacon, pancakes, hashbrowns, grapes, strawberries, everything breakfast. A jug of orange juice sits in the center of all the food, with glasses and coffee mugs.

"Oh, it smells good here, Cap!" A man's voice coming from behind startled me, making me flinch. A tall, burly man grazes my right shoulder, b-lining to the food table. His light brown hair is still messy from sleep. He has a hoodie and basketball shorts with "CWFD" on them. Three other men follow behind, two wearing sweats, the other wearing his uniform. Neither of them paid attention to me, standing in the kitchen like a scared cat surrounded by dogs. They're all so much taller than me and far more muscular. A few more guys join the table for the feast. Only one is looking in my direction. I am standing here awkwardly holding my bag, which probably weighs as much as I do, in my uniform bottoms and hoodie with a ball cap covering my bed head.

"Well, come on, probie, get some protein before shift."

Caption Kelso waves his muscular arm over all the food before him. His dark, slicked-back hair shone in the light above the table, and his strong jaw flexed with every bite he took.

One of the guys nearly spits out the orange juice he just took a sip of and looks up to me.

"You're the new probie?!" He shouts

"I am," I say shyly.

"Holy shit!" He laughs. "I thought you were office staff."

"Boys, this is firefighter Dovetch. Please welcome her like one of our own." Captain Kelso's voice is soft, but he doesn't take his eyes off his coffee.

"Dovetch?" Another guy asks. "Like, chief Dovetch?"

"He was my dad."

The room fell silent for a moment. Each head at the table slumped down or looked up at another. Years after the incident, the fire department still considers it a sensitive subject.

"He was a good man." Captain Kelso says softly. Every head at the table only nods. The silence lingered.

"This is the quietest I have ever seen a bunch of firefighters." A man's voice breaks the silence from behind me. I turn around, the momentum of my bag causing me to lose my balance. I stumble to regain my footing when two strong hands grasp my shoulders. I meet eyes with possibly the most beautiful man I have ever seen. His black hair was pushed to the side with a few stray strands over his brows, and his dark eyes were nearly black, the polar opposite of my icy blue. His golden, tan skin is accompanied by dark stubble lining his sharp jawline.

"You good?" His rough voice echoes through the kitchen, vibrating all my senses and chilling my spine.

I nod my head as I stand back up straight. Laughter comes from behind me.

"Her bag is as heavy as she is!"

"Austin, enough." Captain Kelso says roughly.

Austin cowers to the words.

"What brings you here, detective?"

Detective? Thank god he isn't a firefighter. The amount of nerves he Is causing deep in my stomach would be a major distraction on a day-to-day basis. His hands linger on my shoulders momentarily before patting me and heading over to the table to steal a slice of bacon.

"Just on a case, thought I would stop by and say 'hey' to my favorite fire boys."

"Need me to autograph the firefighter calendar for you? I'll even add a lipstick mark for you. It just won't be from my lips."

"Eddie, come on. There's a lady present."

The detective looks at me and lets out a chuckle. "That would be a pretty small mark, then. Might not even notice it."

The whole table, but Eddie laughs. Austin nearly spits out his food.

"So what's the case, Colson?" Captain Kelso asks the detective. Of course, he has a hot name like Colson.

He finishes chewing his piece of bacon before answering.

"There was a body found on a construction site. They're tearing down the old library to rebuild. A young woman completely mutilated. Poor thing looks like she was tortured before she finally passed."

"That's too bad," Kelso says.

"It looks like she was killed somewhere else and then dumped at the old library in the hope that the building would be torn down before anyone noticed. Luckily and unluckily, they did a last walk-through before beginning the final demolition. The poor guy who found her was traumatized. Threw up and everything."

"Her body was that bad?" I chime in. All eyes turn to me and then back to Colson.

"Oh yeah," Colson says, taking another bite of bacon. "Multiple stab wounds, her abdomen was cut wide open, and it looks like some acid was injected into her neck, eating away at her. Her eyes were missing, too. Very gruesome scene. Even our top detective got sick just looking at her."

What kind of monster would do something like that to an innocent woman? Injecting acid? You have to be fucked up in the head to do that to another human being. My stomach twists just thinking about it.

"I didn't catch your name." Colson snaps me out of my train of thought.

"I'm Codi," I say, stepping closer and extending my hand to him. "Codi Dovetch."

He smiles and takes my hand in his, shaking it firmly. His white teeth shine bright under the kitchen lights.

"Dovetch?" He asks, still gripping my hand.

"Yeah, like Chief Dovetch. He was my dad."

"Ah," he says, releasing his grip. I'm so sorry to hear what happened. He is a legend. Much respect to him."

"Thanks. It was a long time ago."

"I'm glad to see one of his kids is following in his footsteps. We need more firefighters like him. Unlike these lazy asses that spend more time comparing dick sizes than doing their job."

"Whoa, whoa!" One firefighter says. Austin tosses a pancake at Colson, hitting his shoulder. I let a chuckle escape. Just then, the tone goes off.

"Station 31, respond to 2032 Southeast Oak Street for a lift assist. An 82-year-old male has fallen in the shower, and his wife cannot lift him."

The female voice over the speaker announces. The guys all grunt and bring themselves to their feet, grabbing one more bite or sip of coffee before heading to the bay.

"Alright, Probie. Let's head out," Kelso says, patting my shoulder as he walks past, leaving me alone with Colson for a moment.

"I'm Colson Delose, by the way." He says as I start to take a step away.

"Nice to meet you, Colson. Good luck with that case. I hope you find the sick bastard who did it."

"Thanks, I'll see you around?" He asks, waving goodbye.

"I hope so," I say, waving back and opening the door to the truck bay.

He flashes a smile at me and nods. "I do, too."

CHAPTER

2

Arriving at the man's home, his wife meets us outside. She takes me by the hand as the first one out of the engine.

"Oh dear, he fell in the shower. I'm not strong enough to pick him up, and I think he might have broken some ribs. He just had a hip replacement not too long ago, and he's on blood thinners."

I take her hand, trying my best to comfort her.

"Don't worry, we're here. We'll take good care of him." I say, reassuring her. Captain Kelso makes his way to my side as I pass the frail, scared older woman off to Austin, who wraps his jacket around her to keep her warm in the cool fall air.

"Whatcha got?" Cap asks.

"82-year-old male slipped in the shower, possible rib fracture, recently had a hip replacement and is on blood thinners currently. Probably a good idea to call medical to check him out." It all comes out so confidently.

"Good job." He responds, ushering me into the house.

We go through the living room and to the bathroom down the hall.

"Help. Please!" The older man shouts from the bathroom.

I'm the first to reach the door to find the poor older man slumped over the tub, half in water, half out. They didn't bother to turn the water off. It had run cold. My instincts take over.

8

It's my time to prove that I am my father's daughter. Shutting off the water, I turn to cap and demand him to find towels. He looks at me, confused as to why I am bossing the boss around, but he listens. It's almost like he wants to see exactly how I work instead of telling me to stay in my lane. He leans out the door to yell at one of the guys.

"Cas! Go get the blankets out of the truck." He commands before searching for more towels for the poor man.

I lean to his level and place my hand on his shoulder blade. He's so cold. He is completely naked, with suds and ice-cold water covering him.

"My side hurts bad." His hoarse voice echoes in the tub.

Cap hands me a pile of towels, and I quickly place them over the man's hips to give him a little more dignity. It's bad enough that he fell in the shower, he doesn't need a bunch of strangers and the new girl staring at his junk.

"Let's get you up, okay?" I say softly to him.

The man nods and takes my hand, which I have held out for him. Even his hands are cold. Cap comes to the other side of the older man and assists him to his feet. Just then, Cas comes in with a large blanket and hands it to me. I toss the blanket over the older man's shoulder and pull it tight over his chest.

"Alright, we're gonna step over the tub, okay?" I direct the question to both the man and Cap. They both nod. His left foot was successfully on the floor outside the shower. Then, the right foot. We lead the older man out of the bathroom and down the hall. As we enter the living room, we are met with the EMTs entering the home. The man's wife stands outside the door in Austin's arms, looking like a picture-perfect firefighter. One that everyone imagines when you talk about a hero. Taking the clothes off his back to keep this stranger warm and comfortable. He stands much taller than the frail women- the muscles of his arms are almost too big for his t-shirt to handle. His light brown hair -which was messy when I first saw him- is now tamed down and lying perfectly. His jawline was covered in the same brown scruff.

"82-year-old male slipped in the shower. He is complaining of side pain and a possible rib fracture. Skin is cold and clammy. He's on blood thinners and recently had a hip transplant." I informed the EMTs as we set the man down on his recliner. I adjust his blanket to cover him up, wrapping my arms over his shoulder. He takes my hand in his and pulls it close to his chest.

"Thank you, dear." His eyes drifted to my name embroidered on the jacket I had thrown over my hoodie. "Your father would be so proud."

Tears build up behind my eyes, but I hold them back. I place my other hand over his and nod to him.

"These kind people will take care of you from here. Put a gripping mat in that tub, okay? I don't want to have to see you hurt again."

The older man smiles and nods as the EMTs take over, getting his blood pressure.

We leave the home and pass the older woman on her way to her husband's side.

"Thank you so much!" She shouts.

We only nod and wave as she disappears into the house. On the way back to the engine, Cap grabs me by the arm, stopping me in my tracks. My heart drops. I'm going to get scolded now for taking charge. I should have just let him take control. It's the first day, and I'm already about to get in trouble.

"Good job. That was impressive for your first call. Most probies forget every basic thing on their first call, no matter how minor."

"Thank you, sir."

"Keep it up. And you'll be great like your father was."

For the number of times I got yelled at in the academy for taking charge, the compliment was unexpected. My dad taught me so much growing up that I breezed through the written portion of the academy. The physical portion was the one I struggled with the most. There's not a whole lot I can do about how small I am and the fact that I bruise just by someone looking at me.

The ride back to the station was quick. The guys talked the whole way back while I stared out the window recapping.

Your father would be so proud.

The words echoed in my head. I had never met that man, yet he knew my dad. Everyone seems to know my dad. I knew he was known around the department, but only in some places. He was always humble about his work, never talked it up, or made himself sound like the hero. The only times I would hear about how great he was was at Christmas parties the stations would put on for the firefighters and their families or when his fire buddies would come around. Otherwise, he was just my dad—just an average family man. I hope to live up to the family name.

The rest of the shift was simple calls. More lift assists, a couple of medical calls, and one or two car accidents. Night fell quickly, and another storm roared outside the station. After dinner, we decided to get some sleep because storms are known to bring on way more emergencies. The twin-size bed is surprisingly comfortable, the room is dark except for a few lighting flashes outside the window, and the station is quiet. I pull the blanket I brought from home up over my chest. I take a deep breath and try to relax my body enough to fall asleep.

I am jolted awake by some thunder. I lay on my side with a bit of drool on my pillow. I better clean that up before the guys find out about it. I'd never hear the end of it for the rest of my career. I tap on my phone to see the time is 2:45 a.m. I managed to sleep a few hours. I lay back down to get more sleep when the tones go off.

"Rescue 31, respond to Creek Hill for a young female who fell in the canal In need of a rescue. Possible leg injury. Police en route due to a report of an attempted kidnapping. Proceed with caution."

I jump to my feet and quickly throw my boots on. Never changing out of my uniform helps to save time. I'm the first one to make it into the bay to grab my rescue gear. Each of the guys file in one by one.

The storm has picked up even more since I fell asleep. The rain is coming down like a monsoon. It's nearly impossible to see out of the windshield of the engine. I'm not sure how the driver can even know if we are still on the road. With how often the lightning strikes, it looks straight out of a movie, blinding me every time. My rescue helmet tightly fastened, pushing my hair down over my brows. Pulling up to the location, three cop cars are parked on the roadside, lights flashing. Again, I'm the first one out of the truck. I follow Cap over to the sergeant on the scene.

"A 25-year-old female fell down the side of the canal trying to run from a strange man she thought was chasing her. It's hard to hear her over the wind and rain. But dispatch said the victim may have broken her leg in the fall."

"Copy that. Dovetch, get suited up. You're heading down there." Cap shouts over the storm.

"Are you sure, Cap?" I shout back.

"If a man were chasing her, she'd be more willing to talk to another female. So you're going down."

I nod and head back to the truck to strap on the harness as the boys get the ropes ready. Once the harness is on tight, Cap hands me a spare harness.

"You're going to have to hook her up in this. We won't risk taking the basket down in this wind."

"Yes, sir!" I shout to him.

Looking over the edge of the canal, I see a thirty-foot drop. The young girl lies on the edge of the water, obviously in pain and very scared. Even I can see that through the rain. Austin grabs me by the harness and hooks me in.

"Be careful, probie. This isn't the best weather for your first rescue."

"Got it. Everything will be fine."

"Don't jinx it now," Cas shouts, passing by.

I lean back over the edge. We learned repealing in the academy, but nothing truly prepares you for the real deal. Taking the first step is difficult as the wind blows my tiny body around. I push through the instinct to *not* seat myself over the edge. It would have been safe to send one of the guys down, but I won't argue with orders yet. I must prove I can follow orders and keep up with everything on probation.

The rain is cold on my face as I begin my descent.

Hop, land, hop, land.

Each hop sent me a few feet closer to the victim. My right hand served as a break when my boots hit the stone wall. I can feel my hand getting warm from the friction. I close my eyes to focus on repealing. Soon, I feel my boots hit the bottom. I hear faint sobs from my right. I unhook my harness and make my way to the sound. A young girl lays on her side, crying and holding her knees to her chest. My headlamp illuminates her, exposing the bruises on her face and arms and an obviously broken tibia puncturing through her skin and jeans. Her thick jacket is soaked in mud and blood. Her long blonde hair was covered in leaves and dirt. Lines run down her face where the tears have washed away the dirt. I make my way to her side, ripping my jacket off to wrap around her cold body. She wraps her arms around my neck and holds me tight.

"I got you. It's okay." I say, insuring her.

She sobs into my neck.

"Here, we need to get this harness on you to send you to my guys. They're going to take good care of you, I promise."

She leans back and nods her head, still sobbing. This poor girl. I get her to her only good foot and hook her to the harness.

"Dovetch, we're only going to be able to pull you up one at a time." My radio calls out.

"Copy. Sending the patient up first."

"Copy that."

I nod to the girl as I hook the rope to her harness.

"Hold on tight, okay?" I shout over the rain.

She nods and grips my hand tight.

"Alright, pull her up!" I shout into my radio.

"Copy! Pulling her up."

Her feet leave the ground, and she holds onto my hand as she pulls into the air.

"It's going to be okay!" I shout to her as our hands get torn apart.

She keeps her eyes on me for a moment but then looks up to the other side of the canal. Her expression becomes even more terrified as she stares off into the darkness—fear building increasingly in her eyes.

My brows push together in confusion. I follow her gaze to the other edge. My headlamp illuminates the edge to see what looks like a person disappearing into the shadows. I stare off in that direction for what feels like a few seconds until I hear shouting from above me.

"Codi! Let's go!" Austin shouts to me over the storm.

I look over to see the rope back down to my side, swaying in the wind, hitting my shoulder.

I hook up my harness and give it two tugs. I look upwards as the rope tugs me off the ground, then back to the spot where I saw the person to see nothing but trees, rain, and darkness.

As I near the top, Cas holds his hand to assist me up over the edge. He helps unhook me and ushers me back to the truck.

Cap meets me there and hands me a blanket since I gave my jacket to the girl. He nods to me, then walks back towards the guys packing the ropes.

"Hey stranger, nice save."

I turn to the voice behind me as I drop my helmet off my head, allowing my hair to collect the rain.

"One hell of a first day, huh?" Colson says.

He stands, slightly slumped over as the rain pelts the top of his head, beading off this rain jacket.

"Yeah, I guess you could say that." I chuckle. "What brings you here?"

"The girl mentioned something about a man attempting to kidnap and assault her. My chief sent me here to see if it's tied to my murder case in any way."

"Ah." I can't help but let my eyes wander back to the other side of the canal.

"Everything okay?" Colson asks, following my gaze.

"Yeah, I just..." I pause.

I meet his eyes again to see his eyebrows raised, waiting for me to continue.

"The girl looked over there real scared. When I looked too, I thought I saw someone walking away. It could have just been my eyes messing with me since I was asleep not long before this."

He nods his head, looking back to where I saw the person. "I'll note that. I'll have some officers search the area just to be safe."

He smiles at me, pats my shoulder, and then heads towards the ambulance where the girl is being cared for. A weird feeling builds in my gut as I gaze back to that area—still empty, hoping it was just my eyes messing with me. It has been a long day, and I am only running on a few hours of sleep, along with all the stress today has brought.

CHAPTER

3

I flip on my fireplace to warm up my tiny apartment. It feels good to sit on my couch, which I got off Facebook marketplace, with a hot cup of coffee, a cozy blanket, and a good book. The rain let up to a light sprinkle outside, but the fog still lingers over the tall buildings. With this weather, Clearwater is beginning to look a lot like Seattle.

My first shift went much more smoothly, but I had more action than expected. I'm still chilled from being out in the storm. I hug my coffee mug for warmth. My eyes drift to my phone on the coffee table, and I can't resist scrolling. I check every social media account when an idea pops into my head. I can't stop myself. I click on the search bar and type in the name.

Colson Delose.

When I click on his name, his profile pops up immediately. He looks beautiful in his profile photo in the driver's seat of his truck, and his smile is bright even in photos.

Work: CWPD.

Lives in Clearwater, Washington.

From: Seattle, Washington.

Relationship status: Single.

I scroll through his photo album. There are family photos from last Christmas—even his family is beautiful. There are photos of when he used to box for fun, his arms and chest glistening with sweat. I scroll down further to find shirtless pictures of him at what I assume is the gym. He has highly defined abs, his arms are toned, his hair is wet from sweat, and his shorts are pulled down just enough to expose a perfect V-line pointing directly down to his...

Oh god, no. Stop it.

I throw my phone to the other side of my couch. I shouldn't be looking at those kinds of photos. He is practically a coworker. The thoughts that raced through my mind while looking at that photo were wildly inappropriate. It's been so long since I've been laid that my imagination has taken over too much. After Trevor, I haven't been emotionally available enough even to go out and meet anyone to bring home. That and I have been just too exhausted after academy to even think about sex. My career has taken over my life, and that is what I need to focus on. Not fucking the first handsome guy who shows me any bit of attention. I must be ovulating. My hormones are just making me crazy.

Yeah, that's it.

I need a shower and a nap. That will help. Maybe even going for a run.

I lie back, close my eyes, and listen to the electric fireplace's artificial crackle and the rain's slight patter. Car horns and sirens echo down the main street. All sounds drift away as I soon fall asleep.

I woke up hours later, still in the same position I had fallen asleep. My neck is stiff from the odd position I'm in. I twist my head, cracking my cervical spin and stretching my muscles. The sun is starting to set. I've been sleeping here all day. My body is sore and stiff. I stand to my feet to stretch out my back. The rain has stopped for a while. It's the perfect time to run.

I put in my headphones to drown out the city life around me. The cold air stings my nose as I step out. For the first half mile of my run, my body protested hard at the movements, screaming, "Just let me rest," repeatedly.

The hospital is just up ahead. I can see people walking in and out of the emergency room when I see a familiar face.

Oh, god. Not now. Not when I'm trying to ease the horny thoughts.

"Hey!" Colson's lips move as he makes eye contact with me.

Damn it.

I should have gone the other way. As I get closer, I plaster on a smile, taking out one headphone to hear better.

"You live around here?" He asks.

"Uh, yeah. About a mile that way," I say, pointing behind me. His eyes drift that way and then back to mine. "What brings you to this area?" I ask.

"Getting statements. We have reason to believe that the girl you saved last night might be tied to the murder. She has some similar injuries to the first victim. Just a better outcome."

"Wow," I say softly. "Well, I hope you find the guy. If you ever need any outside help, let me know." I chuckle.

Stupid. Why would you say that? You know nothing about his job. You can't help him at all. Idiot.

The voice in my head whispers over and over. A smile grows on his face, and I realize I've been smiling like an idiot.

"I may take you up on that someday. Have a nice night. I'll see you around!" he says, heading toward his car.

I wave him goodbye. I notice him glance back and smile at me.

Damn it.

His smile is hypnotizing.

No, stop.

He is a coworker—nothing more than that. I am just hormonal, that's all. Dylan's wife, Claire, was right.

Stay away from the handsome firefighters and cops. They're tricky.

I need to listen to my sister-in-law. Then again, she did marry my oldest brother. I am still determining how smart she is.

I extend my run a little longer, trying to clear dirty thoughts from my head. I debate whether I should head home to my vibrator and take a long, hot shower. Maybe that would help my mind calm down.

I spent the rest of my two days off resting and going for runs. I can't even count the number of movies I watched in those 48 hours and the amount of take-out food I had eaten. But, it did feel good to walk back into the station for my second shift, my uniform clean and dry. I'm hit in the face with my jacket from the other night.

"That girl wanted me to thank you for giving her your jacket. She was extremely grateful," Cap says, handing me a cup of freshly made coffee.

"Thanks," I say softly.

He nods and heads to the table where Austin and Cas eat eggs.

"Hey, Dovetch!" Austin shouts. "Come sit with us."

I drop my bag in the living area and go to the table. Cas slides over a plate and a large bowl of scrambled eggs.

"Where the hell is Leo?" Cap asks.

"Right here, cap," Leo says, walking through the door. "Sorry, traffic was ridiculous. I swear people forget how to drive in this weather."

Cas lets out a loud chuckle with a mouth full of food.

"So how about that save the other night," Austin says, nudging my arm. "Crazy first day."

"Tell me about it," I respond, taking a sip of coffee.

The morning was slow, leading into the evening. There were only a few lift assists and a traffic collision that was more of a fender bender. The sun is about to set as we all sit in our recliner, watching whatever Cas decided to put on. I didn't argue about anything he decided since I had my book. Romantic, fantasy smut was better than anything the guys chose. Just as I finish up my chapter, the tones go off.

"Station 31 Delta response to a structure fire at an apartment building at 1830 Main Street. Multiple victims were reported inside. Rescue unit requested. Police and medical en route."

Now we're talking.

It's an actual fire. As exciting as the rescue and some car crashes were, I've been waiting for my first fire.

I put my turnouts on in record time, hopping into the back and quickly latching on my SCBA. The adrenaline has set in as we get closer to the fire. I look out my window to see flames lighting up the surrounding area. The fire is massive, much bigger than I expected.

"Alright, Cas. I need you to run the hydrant. Austin, get on the ladder and start spraying that smoke and knocking down the flames. Leo and Codi, you two are going in for the rescue. Two were reported on the third floor trapped in apartment 320."

"Copy." We all say together.

Austin jumps out first, holding his hand like a gentleman to help me. We all quickly turn on our tanks and double-check each other before heading to the fire. Leo grabs my jacket and hands me a Halligan tool before we head inside.

The smoke covers the ceiling, still high enough to walk through upright. I feel a pat on my right arm and see Leo pointing to a door with a sign that reads *stairs* next to it. I nod and follow his lead.

My legs begin burning and protesting only one flight up, but my adrenaline is so high I push through the pain. The smoke gets heavier and heavier the further we ascend. Leo sends his shoulder into the third-floor door, sending it flying open, exposing flames and smoke. The fire alarms blared so loud we almost missed the call of the victims behind the door of apartment 320.

"Step back from the door!" Leo shouts to the people calling for help, then takes his axe and slams the head of it into the door, breaking it off the hinges. A man and a woman come running out, coughing and gasping for air. I grab the man's arm and lead him to the stairs, only to find flames devouring it.

"Rescue 31 to Command!" Leo shouts into his radio.

"Command, go ahead." A voice responds.

"We have the victims, but our exit is blocked, and the fire escape is on the other side of the building. Requesting an alternate exit."

"Rescue 31, the ladder truck is positioned on the alpha side window. Break that and get the victims out that way. We have a crew ventilating the delta side of the building to control flow pattern."

"Copy! Heading to alpha side."

Leo waves his hand to his right, gesturing us all to head that way. I give the man a light push to send him in front of me towards the large window at the end of the hall. As we approach the window, I can see Austin at the top of the ladder, waving his arm to have us clear away from it. Leo and I both have the same idea: grab each victim and crouch them down, then cover them to protect them as Austin smashes the large window open.

As the glass falls, I hear strange noises coming from behind us. I look towards the noises to see the flames and smoke getting bigger.

"GO! GO! GO!" Leo screams.

The woman is already on the ladder on her way down. Leo reaches out to help the man as he steps onto the ladder. I hold the man's hand as he climbs on, but the sounds start again. I take a small step back as the man releases my hand—the floor flexes, and then there is a loud pop.

I look up to meet Leo's eyes before I'm sent through the floor below.

CHAPTER

4

ayday! Mayday! Mayday! Firefighter down. I repeat, firefighter down! Firefighter Dovetch fell through the third floor. The current suspected location is the alpha side, second floor.

The voices over the radio fade in and out. I try to bring myself up to my knees, but my visibility is near nothing. The smoke here is far thicker than it was on the third floor. I feel blindly for the wall, and after a few seconds, my hand hits the sheetrock. I can find my way to the stairs and pray they're not entirely engulfed. I tried calling for help over my radio, but my radio was busted in the fall.

I'm on my own.

I begin crawling along the wall, hoping to find the exit. After what felt like hours, I find the door to the stairs and shove it open. Smoke rolls in, even thicker than when we came through. I can't see flames, so I walk through the door. The visibility is slightly better, but the smoke is still thick and dark overhead.

I need to get moving, and I need to get out of here now. I push down the panic building inside me, remembering my father. Don't freak out. I can't freak out. I need to stay calm. Calm my breathing to save air—deep breath in, slow, humming breath out. I force myself to my feet, both screaming at me to stop. I get to the first step, and I hear something behind me. I turn to look to see what I feared most—a flashover.

The thick smoke ignites through the door, forcing it back wide open and sending a force through me, throwing me off my feet and down the stairs. I roll down to the landing, my body screaming even louder at me. My mom would tell me *I told you so* if she saw me. This situation is the worst case possible. I grunt as I pull myself up again. Fire is above me, and now fire is below me. I'm trapped. I'm going to die here on my first fire. This would be embarrassing if I weren't scared for my life. My dad will kick my ass when I meet him again. Far too early. I'm only 24, for fucks sake.

No. I'm not going to die here. I've gotten this far. I have to keep going. The fire above me is much thicker than the fire below me. The fire started on the second floor, and I'm so close to the exit. I have to fight through it. A few burns are better than death.

I grab the railing and follow it down to the first-floor door. The flames are whipping through the door that is still open from when we came in. I grab the door frame, attempting to pull myself through, when that same noise I heard before the flashover starts again. My heart drops to my stomach as flames charge at me like an angry bull. I throw up my arms to block the fire erupting through the door, expecting them to slam into me. But I don't feel a force—just the warmth through my gloves. Confused, I look up to see a wall of flames forming around me, not touching me. I stare at the flames in awe. I moved my hands slightly, and the flames moved with them like they were following orders. I move them again. The flames move along with them.

What the hell?

I bring my hands together, then split them apart. The flames separated, creating a path. I stand, shocked. I should be dead. My body should be burning to a crisp right now. I should be meeting my dad in the afterlife. But I'm here, and the flames are… listening to me. Like, I am their master. I take a step, and the open path grows longer. I take a few more steps, the path clears more. I need to ignore whatever is happening momentarily, get out, and ask questions later. Continue through the path the fire is clearing for me, retracing my steps from when I came in with Leo. A moment later I can see the front door and firefighters outside scrambling. Cap is standing by the engine, shouting commands when Cas grabs his arms, bringing his attention to me, now walking through the front glass door.

"Dovetch!" He screams, almost panicked.

Cas, Austin, and Leo run to my side, ushering me to the rehab unit. Paramedics scramble to me, ripping off my now melted mask and helmet. The fire was so hot that everything was ruined. One paramedic begins ripping my turnouts off. I look down, expecting my skin to be black and blistered, but it's the normal pale tan it was when I entered the fire. Not a burn in sight. I see the paramedics look at each other, confused, before strapping an oxygen mask to my face. The cool oxygen is a relief. A poke on my arm catches my attention as one paramedic starts an IV.

"Dovetch, how are you feeling? Any burns? Broken bones? Anything?" Cap asks franticly.

I shake my head, and he looks at me confused. I pull my mask down to explain more.

"I'm just a little sore from falling a few times. Other than that, I feel fine. I can head back in."

"No." Cap orders.

"But cap, I feel fine."

"Codi, there were two explosions in that building. You were in the middle of both of them. You should be dead, if not seriously injured. You're going to the hospital to get checked out. No arguments."

I nod as he forces my oxygen mask back up on my face. The paramedics lay me down on the gurney, and we make our way to the hospital.

The hospital released me almost immediately, stating there were no burns or lung damage found. They gave me a few painkillers for some bruised rips from falling down the stairs. The doctor gave me a clean bill of health so I can head back to work. I walk to the waiting room to find the guys and Cap waiting for me. They each jump up when they see me walk through the door.

"A clean bill of health," I announce.

They all smile, one by one, patting my shoulder as they pass by. Leo stops in front of me and pulls me into a tight hug.

"I thought I watched you die." He whispers in my ear before releasing me and joining the other guys. A hand falls on my shoulder, and I see Cap.

"I'm glad you're okay." He says.

A half smile grows on my face. "Yeah, me too," I say, joining him back to the truck.

Back at the station, I recognized a car parked in the front parking lot. As we walk in, my suspicion is confirmed when I see Colson sipping coffee at the table. He jumps up, nearly tipping the chair back when we open the door.

"Hey, I saw the news. Firefighter down?"

His eyes drift to me as I walk out into the opening. Austin grabs me by the shoulders and shakes me slightly.

"Yeah! This chick fell through the third floor, leaving the fire without a scratch. Can you believe that?"

Colson's eyes drift from Austin back to me. His brows push together after he examines me, obviously confused that there are no scratches or burns in sight.

"Alright, boys. Give her some space. Why don't we go get some rest and let Codi calm down a bit."

"Yes, Cap." The guys groan before disappearing into their bunks.

And then I was left alone with Colson.

"I don't think I can sleep now." I chuckle as I go to the fridge for a water bottle.

"How are you feeling?" Colson's deep voice comes from behind me.

I pause before facing him, now leaning on the kitchen island.

"Great. A little sore, but good."

A moment of silence falls between us. I decide to go to the table when my arm is grabbed, and I'm stopped.

"Codi." My name leaving his lips sent a chill down my spine. "How did you make it out of that fire?"

I meet his eyes and respond with a shoulder shrug.

"I saw the footage of you coming out of that building. There were two explosions. Your gear was completely melted and burnt to a crisp. You should be dead."

"So I've been told," I grunt, pulling my arm out of his grasp and continuing to the table, sitting in my usual chair at the head of the table. Colson rushes over to the chair next to me, leaning in closer.

"Codi, seriously, you should be dead. Or hurt. Or something. That fire was huge. But you came out like a miracle. What happened?"

I take a sip of water before meeting his eyes again. His deep brown eyes show every emotion he feels, and a look of concern floods them. I take a deep breath.

"I handed off one of the victims to Leo, I fell through the floor, I got up and crawled to the stairs, and made my way out. That's it."

The look on his face tells me he doesn't believe a word I just said. I hold eye contact, raising my brows as I sip more water. He grabs the bottle out of my hand and sets it on the table.

Confusion floods me, still holding my hand up like the bottle is still there.

"What really happened."

"I just told you."

"That's not everything." He says softly.

My brows push together again. "Why does it matter?" I ask.

"It's a miracle you made it out alive, let alone unharmed." His voice is deep and soft.

"I'm not completely unharmed."

Now, his brows push together.

"My ribs hurt. I think I broke a nail, too," I say, raising my hand to view my Unmanicured nails.

He grabs my hand and brings it down to the table. A chill is sent up my spine again, and the butterflies start having a rave in my gut. We both glance down at our hands joined together. He quickly releases.

I take another deep breath and look around the empty room.

"You wouldn't believe me if I told you." My eyes meet his again.

"Try me." He says softly.

"You're going to think I'm insane."

He leans closer. "Try me." He whispers.

I sigh, lean back into the chair, and then bring myself down to lean on the table closer to him.

"Okay," I sigh. "I handed off the man to Leo, and I fell through the floor and crawled to the stairs."

His face drops like I'm lying again.

"Hold on." I throw my hand up. "As I got to the stairs, a flashover threw me down the stairs. That's where I hurt my ribs. I got up and followed the railing down to the first floor. When I got to the door, there was another flashover. I put my hands up to block my face and.." I pause.

"And?" He whispers.

"And the fire listened to me."

His brows push together again. "What do you mean it 'Listened'?"

"It listened. Like, it went around me. And then I parted it and made my way out without getting burnt. I don't know how to explain it. It just happened. Like, I controlled the fire."

Our eyes lock for a moment, and his laughter breaks the silence. My brows rise. His laughter begins to fade, and my face stays solemn.

"You're joking?" He chuckles.

I shake my head slowly, and his face drops.

"You're serious."

I nod.

"How."

"If I knew, I'd tell you. But even I can't figure it out."

Colson leans back in his chair, one arm resting on the table. His jaw flexes like he's about to say something but stops himself. I stare at him, practically watching the gears turning in his head.

"Now I see why you expected me to think you were crazy."

I let out a light chuckle as I reached for my water.

"Because you do," I whisper.

His eyes lock on me, and he places his hand on mine as I set down the water bottle. I bring my eyes to his.

"I don't." He says softly. "I don't think you're crazy at all."

I look from his eyes to our hands, then back to his eyes.

"Go get some rest. You look like you need it."

"Gee, thanks." I laugh.

"I didn't mean it like that. You look beautiful."

His words twist my gut again as he stands and leaves the station.

Laying in that same twin-sized mattress, his voice echoes in my head.

You look beautiful.

I haven't heard anyone say that since my dad. My brothers love me but never compliment me like that—quite the opposite. I'm sure he only said that because the comment, "You look like you need it," came off as an insult. But I can still feel his hands on mine. Soft and smooth, warm, comforting. I try to shake the feeling off and reflect on what happened tonight. Any possibility I can think of doesn't explain how the fire acted. Everyone is right. I should be dead right now. The fire marshal should be knocking on my family's doors right now, breaking the news. Claire would probably cry the most. She came into my life at a young age and has treated me like her sister. My brothers would hold back any tears to look strong for their wives and kids. Mom probably expects it and has been preparing herself for that knock at the door since I applied. Jack, Hayden, and Carter. My three nephews. They are still too young to understand why Aunt Codi isn't there for Christmas.

My mind races for hours before I finally drift off to sleep, allowing my body to relax.

CHAPTER

5

It's been a few weeks since I last saw Colson. He hasn't stopped by the station once. Flashbacks of the last time I talked to him pop up occasionally, making me wonder if he only said those things to make me feel better. I bet he does think I'm insane. I would think he was if he told me he controlled fire with his mind. So, I guess I don't blame him.

As I walk in the door of the station, I hear laughter. I walk in, set my bag down, and head to get coffee without looking up.

"Hey, there she is!" Leo calls out from the table.

"Morning," I grumble.

"You alright?" That voice makes my head whip over to find Colson standing by the head of the table where I usually sit.

I'm shocked to see him. His scruff has grown a bit more since I last saw him. His smile grows as our eyes meet, but there's still concern behind his eyes.

"Uh, yeah. I'm alright. Just a little tired, is all."

Colson nods slowly, but it looks like he doesn't believe that's all. I take my bag and coffee to my bunk to avoid a more awkward conversation. As I set my bag on the bed, I hear a knock on the door frame. I look over to see Colson leaning against the frame.

"You sure you're okay?"

I nod.

"So You uh…" he pauses, looking at the floor. "You control any more fire lately?" He asks nervously.

I clear my throat before answering. "I haven't, no. Haven't been trapped in a life or death situation lately."

He lets out a scoff.

"Find any more murders?" I try my best to change the subject.

"There's been three."

My brows raise. "Three?!"

"All the same injuries, same causes of death, similar locations, abandoned buildings."

"Any suspects?"

He shakes his head. "No, not yet."

His mouth opens like he's going to say something else, but just as he does, the tones go off.

Saved by the bell.

"Station 31, respond to a house fire at 367 Southeast Grant Street. Possible victims inside."

"That's your queue, miss hero."

I chuckle at the nickname before making my way to the trucks.

Driving through the residential neighborhood, I can see the smoke filling the air. Multiple people gather on the street to watch the blaze. The two-story multifamily home stands tall, flames shooting out the second-story windows. As we get out of the truck after hearing our orders, a woman frantically runs up to Cas, grabbing his jacket.

"Please!" She screams. "My daughter! I think she's still inside! Please save my baby girl!"

Tears run down her cheeks as Cas comforts her. He nods to me.

"What's her name?" I ask the crying woman as I strap on my gear and prepare my new, unmelted mask.

"Abby, her name is Abby. She's only nine." She sobs.

I reach Cap, standing by the incident commander, getting every last detail.

"Cap! There's a nine-year-old girl trapped inside."

He looks at me before shouting for Leo.

"You two go in there and get that little girl out." He shoots his eyes at Leo. "No crazy hero stuff, in and out. And you..." he points to me. "No falling through any floors."

"No promises." I laugh before strapping on the last of my gear and heading in.

The flames flood the back room, I'm guessing the kitchen. The stairs are straight ahead, and smoke is traveling up. The fire has made its way into every room downstairs.

"Abby!" I shout over the roar of the flames.

I hear a faint voice from upstairs. Slapping Leo's arm to get his attention, I point to the top of the stairs, and we begin our climb. Steep, narrow stairs are a fully geared-up firefighter nightmare. The top of the stairs is covered in thick smoke. We each shout for Abby to hear her faint voice from the bedroom down the hall. I use tools to sound the floor as we walk, this time to be safe. I don't exactly want to be known as the girl who always falls through the floor in every fire. We shout her name again to hear her voice behind the door.

"Back away from the door! We're going to break it open!" Leo shouts as he places the Halligan tool between the door and the frame. He gestures for me to hit the tip with my tool to set it in, the metal colliding, ringing in my ears.

He pries open the door to find the room engulfed in flames.

"Abby! Where are you?" I scream.

"Here!" Her voice calls out from the corner of the room.

Leo shoves me toward her voice, and I approach the young girl hiding under a desk. I hold my hand out, and the little girl runs into my arms. I grip onto her for dear life.

"Alright, let's go!" I shout to both the girl and Leo.

Leo is the first to make it through the door, but just as I go to the door with the girl wrapped around me, flames cover the opening, and a bookshelf falls and blocks our exit.

"Fuck!" I curse.

I have the worst possible luck in these fires. I throw my hand up to block the heat of the flames from slapping the poor girl in the face.

"Dovetch!" Leo calls out from behind the flames. Poor guy seems to witness me almost die every time.

"We're good! We'll find another way out! Go!" I shout back to him.

"Command, this is rescue 31," I shout into my radio.

"Command, go ahead." The voice on the other end responds.

"We need to exit through the window. Permission to break the glass."

"Negative, the flow path is too risky."

I look around the room to see no other route. I'll take my chances.

"Leo, do you copy?"

"I copy." Leo's voice chimes through the radio.

"Are you out of the building?" I ask.

"Yes, I'm just now walking out." He responds.

Perfect. I hoist Sarah high on my hip and wrap my left arm tightly around her. I shift my right hand up the handle of my axe and prepare to break the window. I can ask for forgiveness later. I need to return this little girl to her mother. I send the head of the axe through the glass, shattering the entire thing in one hit. I hear a roar come from behind us. I whip around to find a wall of flames heading our way. I shift Abby in front of me and throw myself over her to block the fire from touching her. My first instinct is to throw my arm over my head, expecting flames to lick my hand, but there's nothing, just the heat. Confused, I look up to see the same wall of flames I saw in the apartment building fire. But this time, there's more of a dome around us.

"Whoa." Abby's small voice says from under me.

A small smile grows on my face as I go to stand. The fire moves with me, away from the window and back out the small opening above the bookshelf blocking the door. As I push the blaze away, I hear a ladder hit the side of the building by the window. Cas pokes his head over the window and holds his hand to the young girl. She runs to him, wrapping her arms around his neck. They both make their way down the ladder while I stay back for a moment, watching the behavior of the fire, responding to my every move. As soon as I see Abby touch the safety of the ground and run into her mother's arms, I reach the ladder, still holding a hand up to control the wall of fire pushing against my force. I lower my hand and duck down as I get both feet on the ladder. The flames shoot out the window above my head. I take a deep breath as I descend the ladder.

Back at the station, the shower runs hotter than at my apartment. The hot water caressing my body is so comforting. Every muscle in my back relaxes with the touch of the water. I rest my head against the shower wall and let the water touch me in places I haven't been touched in a long time. I shut my eyes and let my imagination take over.

Hands running up and down my arms, making their way to my breasts, caressing them gently. Smooth hands travel down to my hips, running along my lower waist, sending a tingle to the bundle of nerves down lower, a body pressing up against my backside, and a kiss lightly planted on my neck. I tilt my head to the side to allow more space for those lips to travel as the hands continue to explore my naked body. I completely roll my body to face the wall as the hands travel lower and lower. The body behind me now lightly pushes me against the shower wall. A jagged breath leaves my chest as fingers run down my inner thighs, the lips now lightly sucking at the spot where my neck meets my shoulder. A finger lightly grazes the most sensitive part of my body, and a soft gasp escapes me. My body tenses as the finger moves back and forth, brushing the bundle of nerves. A tight feeling creeps inside as one finger enters me, now two. A light moan leaves my lips as they push in and pull back out over and over, rubbing against me. The lips continue to kiss my neck while the hand makes rhythmic motions in and out. The other hand travels up to my breasts and lightly squeezes. My breath becomes rapid with every movement. I feel him press up against my backside, getting harder with every moan. Feeling the length against me causes every nerve to become more sensitive and the tingling down low to go wild. The fingers move faster, and I feel tension building deep inside.

A moan escapes my lips again as the body behind me presses up harder, sliding my hips back against him. I feel him reposition and slide his way in. I gasp as he fills me. More kisses land, now along my jaw, gently suckling. He moves in and out of me, forcing a moan out with each stroke. His fingers continue the rhythmic motion on that bundle of nerves, sending electricity through my body. The tension deep down builds and builds, wishing to escape. He strokes harder and deeper, filling me with each movement. A moan is forced out as he goes deeper. I'm so close to climax when a whisper comes from my left ear. *Codi.*

Colson's voice snaps me out of my daydream. I spin around to see I'm alone in the shower. I rest against the shower wall and attempt to slow my breath.

Come on, Codi, get a grip. You can't be doing this.

I flash myself with ice-cold water, hoping to calm my thoughts before shutting the water off completely. I wrap myself in a clean towel and then wipe the steam away from the mirror. My dark hair is flat on my forehead, and the little bit of mascara I decided to wear today is running down my cheeks. My skin is still flush. I need to finish this shift, go home, and focus on my job. I splash some more cold water on my face before meeting my own eyes in the mirror again.

"Knock it off, girl. Focus on work. You need to focus on your job." I growl to myself.

CHAPTER

6

I'm the only one awake in the station, leaning back in a recliner with my feet up as some random movie runs in the darkness. All the lights are out except for the one over the sink in the kitchen. We haven't gotten a call in hours. With only six hours left in my shift, I'm taking advantage of having the living area to myself. I flinch when the door clicks open. I thought everyone was in bed. I sit up and turn my head to see who is coming into the firehouse.

Colson strides In, looking down at a file of papers. He glances up momentarily and finds me looking at him, confused.

"Oh, sorry. I didn't think anyone was awake." He says.

"Neither did I," I say, leaning back into my reclining position.

Colson walks over to pour himself a cup of coffee, still hot on the pot, then heads to the dining table. I watch every moment he makes graceful, smooth. I clear my throat and look back to the TV as his eyes drift to me.

"Whatcha watching?" He asks, sitting down in a chair.

"Honestly, I have no idea. The guys started it, then immediately decided to go to bed. I'm just too lazy to change it."

He chuckles as he brings the hot coffee to his lips. I glance back over to him to watch him open his laptop, which I hadn't even noticed he carried in. He spreads a handful of papers across the table. A light snort shoots out my nose, a little louder than I expected.

Colson flings his head in my direction. "What?" He says, amused.

I chuckle as I grab myself a cup of coffee, too.

"Don't take this the wrong way, but... uh, don't you have an office or a home to work in?"

He laughs. "Believe it or not, the firehouse is quieter than my office."

"Well, that is hard to believe." I lean against the counter, sipping on the still-hot coffee.

A long silence falls between us, and I can't help but feel my face heating up, remembering my daydream earlier. I'm knocked out of my thoughts by Colson's coffee mug hitting the table as he sets it down.

"You working on that murder case?"

He nods, not taking his dark eyes off the computer screen.

"How's it coming?" I ask, genuinely curious.

He sighs, rolling his eyes. "I wish I could say good. I'm stumped."

I begin my way back to my recliner when Colson speaks up again.

"Hey," he says. "Remember when you said to let you know if I need any outside help?"

"Yes." I scoff.

He pulls the chair next to him out a bit and pats the seat.

"Can I get some help?"

His pleading smile melts my heart. Seeing him ask for help is almost sad. A chuckle leaves my nose, and I smile.

"Whatcha got?" I ask as I make my way to the chair next to him.

"So far, there are four victims, all beaten, stabbed, abdomen cut open, and acid injected into them. All are left in abandoned buildings, but it looks like they were killed in a different location. There were no fingerprints anywhere and no DNA. I can't seem to find anything. This guy is clean with his kills."

"Do you have the crime scene photos?" The words leave my mouth before I can even think of them.

"I do." He says, weary.

My eyes travel back and forth between him and his laptop.

"Are you sure you want to see them? They're pretty gruesome."

I give him my classic side eye.

"Ok, Ok." He throws his hand up before pulling up some files on his laptop.

"This is the first girl, identified as Jenna Roberts. Twenty-three years old, still in med school. Her mom reported her missing a week before we found her."

The first photo he shows me is a portrait. She's beautiful. Long, light brown hair flowing perfectly over her shoulders, a bright smile, and bright blue eyes slightly squinting from how big her smile is. She looks so happy and full of life—a gold chain necklace standing out against her golden tan skin. I look to Colson, letting him know I'm ready for the next photo. He clicks. The photo switches from a beautiful, bright girl to a horrific sight. My jaw drops. This gorgeous girl was utterly mutilated. Her beautiful blue eyes were now just craters on her face, her full cheeks now bloody and bruised, her gold necklace still on but now surrounded by blistered and burnt skin from the acid along with a large laceration just above the chain, her jaw offset to the side. Obvious rigor mortis set in long before this. I can tell even through photos.

The photo changes again, showing another beautiful soul: long black, shiny hair, almond-shaped deep brown eyes, and the same big, bright smile.

"The second girl, Rebecca Long. 24 years old. A kindergarten teacher reported missing by the school principal when she didn't show up to work."

She's my age.

The photo changes again to another horrific sight. Slouched against the wall, eyes missing, skin blistered and bruised, mouth open slightly with bruises covering her cheeks, her beautiful blue cardigan wholly stained with blood and dirt. My gut twists at the sight. The photo switches again.

"Third girl, Cara Brooks. Twenty-four years old, she works as a part-time waitress and volunteers at the retirement home in her free time. Reported missing by her parents."

This time, she's a blonde-haired girl with bright blue eyes. Her golden skin is covered in silver rings, and her hands have a tiny heart tattoo on her wrist. Bright pink lips surround a bright white smile, and a silver nose ring shines in the light.

Click.

Her screaming face, missing those bright eyes, was lying on her back, hanging off a pallet. Her face was bruised and bloody, her neck blistered and bruised, her throat slashed. Even the nose ring looks less bright.

I take a deep breath before Colson clicks on the next photo.

"And the fourth girl. Rachel Linwood. Also, twenty-four years old."

I interrupt Colson as I recognize her face.

"She was in my class in the academy. She was super sweet."

"Did she quit?"

"No one knew. She just stopped showing up a week before graduation. Chief tried calling her but never got an answer, so we assumed she couldn't do it anymore. She struggled more than I did, so it made sense. The last time I talked to her, she was upset about being unable to make it up the tower with the hose."

Colson's eyes don't leave me as I stare at her photo.

Long dark hair, pin straight, wearing the very academy shirt I last saw her in.

"Are you sure you want-"

"Yes." I interrupt.

Colson takes a breath and clicks. This photo shocks me slightly. This time, her body has been tied to a pole and burnt.

She has the same injuries, but her clothes are burnt to a crisp. Her once-long hair shriveled at the ends. Blood was running from her nose and where her eyes used to be. I take a sharp breath. This girl was the most friendly. She was the only one who spent time with me at the academy. I helped her with the written portion while she tried to work with me on the physical portion. We both struggled but helped each other. We would get there early every day and go for a run before class. She didn't deserve this. The photo vanishes, and I blink multiple times. I look over to see Colson looking at me concerned, one arm resting in front of the laptop.

"The only similarities we can find are the injuries and that every victim is female around the same age. The last victim, obviously some differences."

"Fire," I whisper.

He nods. I take a deep breath in and out my nose, trying to process everything in the photos.

"Can I see the last one again?" I ask softly.

Colson grunts but obliges, and the photo is back on the screen. I scan the photo, looking for what? I don't even know. I fight fires and rescue people, so I don't look for clues. As I'm scanning around the photo, something weird catches my eye.

"May I?" I ask, reaching over to the mouse pad of the laptop.

Colson lifts his hands, surrendering the laptop to me. I slightly lean over him to look closer, zooming into her hand. That ring on her finger seems so familiar. I zoom in closer, but the photo becomes too pixelated to see clearly.

"What is it?" Colson says softly over my right shoulder.

"It's just... It's That ring." I pause. "It looks like one given to me a long while ago." My voice came out breathy.

"Where was it bought?"

A long pause falls between us as I stare at the photo of my old ring on this poor girl's hand.

"It was custom-made. It's one of a kind."

CHAPTER

7

Staring at the suds as they run down the fire department's logo that builds with every sponge swipe, I think back to the photos from the other night. The amount of pain those poor girls must have gone through. All of them seemed like good people, too. A future doctor, a teacher, a volunteer caretaker, and a future firefighter were all taken way too soon. However, the image that sticks with me the most is the ring on Rachel's finger. It looked so much like the one I used to have. My last boyfriend gave me the custom-made promise ring. It wouldn't bother me so much if I didn't return the ring to him the day I left. Is it just a coincidence that Rachel had the same ring? Has it been so long since I saw it that a similar one freaks me out? Water sprays my face, shooting me back to reality.

"You good Dov?" Leo's voice echoes in the bay.

"Yeah," I say, shaking the thoughts from my head. "Just lost in thought."

"Thinking about the detective?"

I flash a confused look his way.

"I'm just kidding. Most girls drool over him all the time. I wouldn't blame you if you did, too."

"I was not thinking about him."

Leo chuckles and continues rinsing the suds off the truck when the tones go off.

"Station 31, respond to a smoke investigation at 745 East Pacific Street. Possible fire inside. The building has been vacant since June."

Leo and I make eye contact before nodding at each other and making our way to the truck.

Pulling up to the location, I noticed a little smoke coming out of the top-floor windows of the two-story building. Its old brick is dirty, and the windows are vandalized.

"Alright, guys… and girl," Cap says over our headsets. "Gear up, and let's check where that smoke is coming from. Be careful, too. It's dark, and who knows what's in there."

The sun was still up enough to give off light, but it set down lower than the buildings, casting shadows in the street. Most of the windows to the building have been boarded up. We throw our SCBAs on and go through the routine of double-checking everyone's gear before heading in. The smoke has traveled down to the first level, making it difficult but not impossible to see. Leo taps my shoulder and points to the stairs in the back. Like every other multiple-level fire, I follow him up the stairs to check out the second floor. Immediately, we see a small fire in the corner of the room. Nothing too big. It is just small enough that Leo puts it out quickly with the extinguisher he brought.

"Fires out, Cap." He calls over the radio.

"Copy that, do a once over to ensure nothing else is in there, then get out of there."

"Copy."

Leo nudges me to take the rooms to the right. The light on my helmet shines through the smoke, and I can barely make out some random chairs and trash lying around. I continue my way around the room. I look up at the walls to see graffiti covering them. Then, I trip over something, sending my body slamming onto the ground.

Fuck

I lift myself and brush the dust off my turnouts. I turn to see what I tripped over. A woman's face, frozen in a scream, gets illuminated by my headlamp. This time, strawberry blonde hair lays fanned out around her, covered in dried blood and dead leaves. Her eyes are missing, blood dripping out of the craters—bubbles of blisters lining her neck. I let out a quick but loud scream. Leo comes running in seconds later, franticly searching for me. He runs to my side, grabs me by the arm, and lifts me to my feet. His light travels down to see the girl, completely naked, cut all over, bruises making up every inch of her body.

"Requesting law enforcement. Dovetch found a body."

I sit on the front bumper as the officers filter in and out of the building. The corner arrived a few minutes ago and is preparing to head in. The guys gave up asking me if I was okay after about the tenth time. I responded, "I'm just fine. Stop asking.".

My turn-out jacket lays on the bumper next to me as I rest my arms on my knees, slouching over in a way that probably isn't that good for my back.

"Codi!" My name is shouted from my side.

I turn to see Colson jogging my way.

"Oh, hey," I call back cheerfully, sitting up straight.

He runs to stand before me, grabbing each of my shoulders.

"Are you okay?!" He says frantically.

I swear if I hear one more person ask me if I'm okay, I will blow up. I take a deep breath before responding.

"Yes, Colson. I am just fine."

He pulls a small flashlight from his jacket pocket, flashing it in my eyes.

"Are you sure?" He says franticly.

Blinded by the small light, I slap his hand away.

"Are you a paramedic now? What are you doing?"

"Did the medics check you out already?"

"Colson." His name came out breathy. "I tripped. That's all. I didn't jump out of the second story. I'm fine."

He stands up straight, reminding me how tall he is. The angle I need to look him in the eyes hurts my neck.

"You found a body. That's traumatic."

I hop off the bumper to stand before him, still having to look up to talk to him.

"Yeah, and I'll probably see much more in my career. It's part of the job." I walk away, unsure where I'm going, but the dramatic effect is worth it.

Colson grabs my arm and swings me around to face him— the obvious shock on my face.

"Did you see anything else? Anything odd."

"Besides you shining a light directly into my retinas, no."

The fact that he's so frantic about ensuring I'm okay confuses me the most. I wasn't the only one who saw the body. I am the one who tripped over it, though. I'll give him that. The poor girl's face is burnt into my memory, but I don't want that to completely traumatize me for the rest of my life. I'll see many more bodies with the career path I took. I can't let the first one affect me so much.

Colson's hand still firmly gripped my left arm, pulling me closer to him. I look down at his hand and then back up to meet his gaze, looking at me with so much concern.

"This is another one, isn't it?" I ask vaguely.

It's a dumb question with an obvious answer. Of course, it's part of the same case. Same wounds, same kind of victim, same kind of location. And the fact that Colson is here, it's all tied together.

He slowly nods at my question. "They're getting more frequent."

We hold eye contact for what feels like hours. His deep brown eyes are almost so dark I can see my ice-blue reflection.

"Stay close to the guys." He says softly. "Until we find this guy. We don't know his motive, but we don't want to take the chance."

His voice is laced with a bit of fear. Fear for me? Does he think I'm next? Could I be next? I don't completely fit in with the rest of the victims. My hair isn't long and beautiful, my smile doesn't brighten the room, and my skin isn't golden and smooth. The only thing I have in common with them is my age. Other than that, I could pass for a twelve-year-old boy if I wear a tight enough sports bra.

"Delose!"

Colson and I turned to where the voice came from, seeing a man waving his arm in the doorway. Colson finally released my arm, letting his fingers softly graze me as they dropped.

"You're free to go." He says firmly.

For some reason, some annoyance erupts inside me with those words, and I can't control the attitude that comes out.

"Gee, thanks. I didn't realize I was being held here against my will."

I definitely get that attitude from my mother. My dad was always firm and assertive with people. But my mom never liked being told what to do, even by my father, who wanted only to keep her safe.

Colson's brows push together, almost surprised at my response.

"Stay with the guys." He repeated, firmly pointing a finger right in my face.

I didn't realize my face showed so much annoyance until I let it relax.

CHAPTER

8

I didn't eat that night. The girl's screaming face burnt into my memory. The image remains there as I sit on my couch, trying to watch holiday rom-coms to clear my head. I only put sweatpants and my fire hoodie on this morning. Take-out boxes are still on my coffee table as the small-town guy confesses his love to the big-city girl on the screen. I suck on my bottom lip, slightly biting it, when there's a knock on my door. I swear to god, if it's Jehovah's Witness trying to convert me again, they're getting a face full of leftovers. I fling my head back and groan as the knocking continues. They're persistent today.

I grunt as I stand and shuffle my way to the door. I unlock the chain and swing the door open to see Colson standing there. Confusion floods my face.

"Hey." He says softly.

"Hey," I say almost more as a question.

"You have a minute?" He asks.

I turn slightly to see the disaster in my apartment. I take a deep breath and clear my throat on the exhale before stepping aside to allow him entry.

"Don't mind the mess," I say as the door shuts.

How embarrassing. The one time he comes to my place, it's a mess. Take out containers everywhere, my fire bag spread like a whore by the washer tucked in the closet, clothes lying everywhere in the bathroom.

Shit.

I think my underwear is on full display in there, too. But then the question enters my head.

"How do you know where I live?" I ask, confused.

He chuckles while glancing around the room. Please don't look at everything. Today was chore day... after the movies, though. Who am I kidding? I was planning on lying around all day, hence the sweats. I never expect company, so I never bother deep cleaning.

"I'm a detective, remember." He chuckles.

"So that automatically makes you a stalker? Got it." I click as I head over to start picking up the trash everywhere.

"No, no. That makes me knowledgeable."

"Whatever helps you sleep at night." The last word comes out with a grunt as I throw my work clothes into the washer.

"Nice place, " he says while looking at the floor-to-ceiling windows. The foggy view of the city below and the dark clouds give it an eerie, ominous feel.

A scoff exits me as I walk to the coffee maker in the kitchen. Reaching for a mug, I pour the still-hot coffee, add some creamer, and then turn back to Colson standing by the window.

"So, what brings you here?" I ask nervously.

We stand in my home, unsupervised and alone. My nerves find a way into my stomach as I think about that, but I play cool, calm, and collected.

"It's about the case." His rough tone bounced off the large windows and then to me. He looks to me for a response only to find me, brows raised, lips pushed against my coffee mug, old sweat pants, and a dirty hoodie. An image worthy of a poster in a teenager's bedroom with a sticky substance on it that no one truly wants to know what it is. Not. If he wasn't standing in my home, I could convince anyone that I was homeless, begging for spare change and crumbs.

Silence falls on us as we hold eye contact for a moment. I nod my head towards the coffee pot next to me.

"Want some?'

"Sure." He says breathy.

I grab another mug, fill it, and slide it across the kitchen island to Colson, who has now sat on the bar stool. As he takes a sip, I take a step to slouch over the counter.

"So, what's up?"

He takes a deep breath before responding.

"That girl you found. She was 18." His eyes met mine. Sadness fills them. "We found her social media. She had multiple dating apps with a false age, all talking to older men. There's one guy she agreed to meet with about a week and a half ago."

"That's great. I mean, not great for her, but great for the case because you found the guy, right?"

He looks down at his coffee and clears his throat. "No. We could see the messages, but he deleted his account before we could search it. Photos and name, all gone."

"So we're back to nothing."

He nods.

"So, You came all the way here to tell me you're still in the same position as the last time I saw you."

His shoulders shrug in response.

"What about the girl from the canal? She must have seen the guy chasing her."

"All she said was that it was dark and it was a man about six foot. He was wearing dark clothes and gloves. She didn't see any facial features or anything distinct enough. She's a dead end."

His eyes darken as he looks down. Disappointed, almost defeated.

"Maybe I should just go for a walk tonight alone as bait." I joke.

"No." His words come out quick and firm, demanding. "You're not doing that."

Something in me recoils at the firmness of his voice, completely submitting to his words. But something else inside me snaps to attention, angry at the demand.

I stare at him from under my brows.

"Stay home or at the station. Keep your doors locked at all times."

My eyes narrow at him as more commands come out of this man's mouth. He meets my gaze.

"Please." He adds.

"Okay," I whisper.

The next few weeks go by slowly. Each shift is less exciting than the last. I didn't wholly mind Colson's request. I walked to and from work and even went to do a little shopping by myself. I doubt the killer is going to come after me. I'm not a stunning, long-haired beauty.

I sit on my couch with a candle on the coffee table. I restlessly stare at the candle, not able to sit still. I stand up and pace, not taking my eyes off the small flame. I bite my bottom lip. The flame dances, taunting me with each movement and swaying side to side exotically. I should take notes to improve my lap dancing technique. In a flash, I slam my weight onto my knees and slide close to the table. The flame was mere inches away from my nose. I stare at the flame with squinted eyes like it's keeping a secret from me. I sigh through my nose and then click my tongue. I look down at my hand resting on my knee and then back to the flame. I bring a finger to the flame, nearly touching it, but I jolt my hand back. What if I was imagining everything?

Screw it.

The voice in my head says. She's a daredevil.

I slowly bring my finger to the flame, brushing it over the tip. The tiny flame wraps around the tip of my finger. I lift my hand a little higher as the flame follows. I raise another finger and watch the flame bounce from one to another, growing a little bigger.

Whoa.

That same daredevil in my head whispers in awe. I tilt my head like a confused dog, watching the flame grow down my fingers, spreading to the rest of my hand. My skin should be blistering by now, pain coursing up my arm, blood boiling. But there's no pain, no smell of burning flesh—just the flames dancing around in the dark of my apartment. The flames grow down my arm, finally reaching the sleeve of my sweater.

Shit!

Panic builds inside me. I'm on my feet in a heartbeat, springing to the kitchen sink and plunging my hand into the running water under the faucet. The flames protest but eventually give up, allowing a cloud of steam to rise to the ceiling. I let out a breath, not even realizing I had been holding it. I slam my hands on either side of the sink and drop my body weight. Okay, I guess I wasn't imagining everything. My singed sweater is proof of that. I flip the faucet back on and splash my face with some water. The clock on the stove reads 9:45 pm. I snort at the clock, completely awake now. Chan's Chinese Food closes at 11 pm, but I still have time.

I brush off what happened, throw on a jacket, grab my keys, and head out the door, disregarding Colson's orders.

CHAPTER

9

The rain started falling lightly again. Chan's is worth a mile walk in the rain, though. Their Beijing beef and chow mien are the best comfort food in town. Anyone who disagrees can fight me any day. I would walk several miles for just a sample size of it. Waving goodbye to Mrs. Chan at the front counter, I enter the light rain. The traffic lights reflect off the flooded streets. Occasionally, a car would drive past. I forgot my headphones back at my apartment for this long walk. I could have ordered delivery, but I needed some fresh air anyway. I take a deep breath, the cold air stinging my nose and a cloud of steam when I exhale.

Stopping at the crosswalk, I glance around the tall buildings decorated with Christmas spirit. They are beautiful. Lights flickered throughout the street, Christmas trees standing proudly in the windows and lobby, and red and green ribbons. I look at the buildings behind me to see something vanish into the shadows. My brows push together when the crosswalk's beeping begins. I take a glance back before continuing down the street.

I make it a few more blocks when I feel someone behind me. I quickly turn to look but see nothing. I'm overthinking, paranoid even. I take a few more steps when something jumps out from the darkness. A man in a trench coat stands in front of me. He throws his jacket open to expose nothing underneath, just straight dick and balls swinging around. He covers up and runs away. So, I guess that's why I felt like someone was following me. I stare blankly ahead of me, trying to process all of that.

"Okay," I say, monotone, before walking again.

That kind of thing isn't shocking in this city. I honestly should have expected it.

I tuck my empty hand deep into my jacket pocket to keep it warm. Black leggings weren't the warmest choice when leaving the house, but here I am, walking down the street in the rain in leggings, duck boots, a zip-up rain jacket, and a beanie. Each step splashes some water up my legs.

Screw this. It's too cold and wet to take the long way. I made a split decision to cut through an alleyway. It should cut 5 minutes off my walk time.

The alleyway is more flooded than the streets and smells like dumpsters full of rotting meat. Walking down the alley's center, I hear footsteps offsetting mine. I slow my footing to listen to them continue their pace. I glance back to see a man a ways away, walking in the same direction as me. His hood is up, and I can't see his face.

You're fine. Just keep walking. It's safe when you're out of the alley. Calm down.

The voice in my head reassures me. I turn back to where I am heading to see it's still a long way. I take a deep breath and pick up my pace a bit. The footsteps get faster, closer. Every time I pick up my speed, the steps match. When I hear them begin sprinting towards me, I take off. I'm not fast enough. My hands grip the arm that was holding my bag of takeout. I swing around, throwing a punch in the stranger's direction. He dodges like he knows my next move. He wears a mask, blocking the details of his face, gloves covering his hands, and everything black. I rip my arm from his grasp, dropping all my food on the wet ground. I try to swing again when a bright light shines on us. He frantically looks up and then sprints in the other direction.

A black Denali screeches to a halt behind me. I turn around to be blinded by its headlights. I throw my hand up to try and block the light when I see a figure making its way to me.

"Get in the truck!" Colson's rough voice burst out of the light.

I nod my head and run to the passenger side. He opens the door for me and slams it when I'm safely inside.

How did he find me? How did he know I would be here?

He climbs in the driver's seat, tires screeching as he throws it in reverse, then flooring it down the street. The engine revved in anger. The attacker is nowhere in sight now.

"What the fuck, Codi?" He shouts.

"What the fuck, Colson?" I shout back. "Were you following me?!"

"It's a good thing I was. You'd be the next victim right now."

"I had it taken care of." I snarl at him—a partial lie.

"Clearly." He growls.

"Don't 'Clearly' me! Why the hell were you following me in the first place? First, you show up at my work multiple times, then at my house when I never gave you my address, and now you show up in some random alley where I'm walking down?"

"You could have been killed." His voice was rough, with a bit of panic and anger behind it. "If I didn't show up when I did-" he pauses. "I'm taking you back to my place. Where you'll be safe."

His place? Alone?

"No!" I squeal.

"I'm not asking." He snarls.

"I don't care if you're demanding it. I'm not going to your place. I'm going home."

He continues driving, ignoring my protests.

"Colson!" I shout.

"You're going to my place where you won't leave my sight, and that's final."

"You can't make me." The childish response slips out.

"I will put you on a fucking leash if I have to."

"Oh, don't threaten me with a good time." The remark came out before I realized it.

"It's not a threat." He growls. "It's a promise."

His hooded eyes meet mine, dark as night.

I gulp a little louder than I wanted to as his eyes drift back to the road ahead. I take a deep breath. There's no arguing with him. The only way I'm getting out of this is if I open the door and roll out now. I try, but the automatic locks are too good. I bite my lower lip, almost puncturing it. I can see in the corner of my eye that he steals a few glances at me.

"I dropped my dinner."

"I'll order you more."

His quick response surprises me.

"My clothes are soaked," I say, leaning towards him.

He's got to let me go home and change, at least.

"I have clothes at home you can wear. I'll run you a hot shower to warm up, too."

I scoff. "I need my phone charger."

"I have one."

Fuck. What else can I use as an excuse to make him let me go home?

"I'm on my period." The words come out so fast.

"I'll buy you tampons."

He's so quick, damn it. There's a solution for everything.

"I don't sleep well on couches."

"You can have my bed."

God, damn it.

"Colson!" I shout. "Let me go home. I'm not staying with you. I'm fine."

"The hell you are." He snarls. "I'm taking you home. End of discussion."

I grunt loudly as I slam my back into the seat. Silence falls on us. The only sounds heard are the engine roaring and the rain pelting the windshield.

"Do you need tampons?" His voice is soft and sincere.

"No!" I shout.

His house is a lot bigger than I expected. A detective can afford more than a one-bedroom apartment. Solar lights line the driveway leading up to a modern-looking home—two tall windows on each side of the front door. Trees surrounding the home giving that quiet, peaceful feel. Even in the rain, it's a beautiful home. Colson parks the truck before the single-car garage and then hops out. I sit for a moment admiring the house when my door is opened. Colson waves an arm like a servant, allowing the queen to pass. I slide out of the truck, still wet from the fight in the rain. He ushers me up the walkway and unlocks the door. The door opens to a large hallway leading to an open floor plan. Much more spacious than my apartment. Floating stairs to my left, living room and kitchen at the end of the hall to the right. Entire floor-to-ceiling windows throughout the home. Purple LED lights line the countertops and TV in the living room. If I wasn't so pissed at him, id be jealous of this place. It's clean. Cleaner than my place.

"Make yourself at home." He says behind me. "I'll go get you a change of clothes, and you can shower upstairs."

I follow him up the steps, gazing at all the art lining the walls. He leads me to his bedroom and digs around the drawers, only to toss a pair of old sweatpants and a white long-sleeved shirt. I see his game with the white shirt. My nipples will decently show through that.

"Bathrooms over there. You can put your wet clothes outside the door, and I'll wash them."

With the clothes in hand, I turn to where he pointed and head for the shower.

The hot water stings my cold skin. Colson has an arrangement of body wash and shampoos sitting perfectly in their assigned spots in the shower. Water beads off the dark tan tiles along the walls. I stare down at the drain, watching the water spin around it when my eyes drift to my right arm. The bruising has started forming on my wrist. Flashbacks of the crime scene photos flash through my mind. Each girl had the same kind of bruising. I am thankful that Colson showed up when he did. Who knows where I would be now? Getting beat? Getting acid injected into my neck? Getting my eyes cut out of my skull? I shiver at the thought. Instead, I'm here in Colson's shower, about to put on his clothes and sleep in his bed. If this gets back to the guys, I'll never hear the end of it.

I dress and head downstairs after I'm nice and warm from the shower. The pitter-patter of my bare feet echoes in the empty hall leading to the living room. I hear rustling around in the kitchen and find Colson unpacking take-out bags. He's wearing dark blue jeans that fit perfectly to his muscular legs, a black zip-up jacket hugging his torso, and dark brown boots still wet from outside. His hair is still damp and lays flat on his brow as he looks down at what he's doing. He spins around and starts messing with something on the counter. My eyes drift down. Damn it, those jeans really hug his ass. As the thought floats through my head, he turns around to find me leaning against the wall, arms crossed.

"Here." He says softly, holding up a cup. "I made some hot tea for you. And I ordered takeout if you're still hungry."

Chan's. How did he know? Has he been following me for so long that he figured out where I'm a regular? If I weren't starving, I would be creeped out. But the smell of Beijing beef chases away any uneasy feeling. He walks over and hands me the cup of tea. The warmth feels so good on my hands. As I pull the cup closer to me, I notice his eyes scanning my wrist. What looks like anger flickers in his eyes, and he turns back to the kitchen in a huff.

"Is this your way of seducing girls? Because it's not working on me." I say, taking a sip of hot tea.

He raises a brow. "Your nipples say otherwise."

I gasp, looking down at my erect nipples nearly ripping through the shirt. I throw one arm over them and search for something to cover up with. A hoodie lays across a chair at the kitchen island. I slam my tea down and throw the hoodie on as fast as possible. He watches me, giggling to himself. I look down to make sure my nipples are invisible to see the Clear Water Police Department logo on the left side of the chest. I grunt in disgust.

"I feel dirty again."

Colson laughs before responding, not even looking up. "Do you need another shower?" He chuckles.

His eyes shoot up to see the hoodie I threw on, then laugh even louder.

"Not a word of this leaves here." I threaten.

"But, you look so good in it."

Yeah, the way too big sweatpants that I can't walk in without stepping on the legs, the hoodie hanging past my thighs. I must look so hot right now.

"I'm going to change, then I'll put on a movie or something. Dig in, " he says, heading for the stairs.

I glance around his home. There are books, lots of books, a large-screen TV with LED lights behind it, and no gaming system.

Green flag.

Everything is clean and tidy, tucked away in its spot.

Green flag.

So far, there's nothing out of the ordinary or alarming. This doesn't look like an advantage, bachelor home. Wondering his living room, I find a lighter sitting on the coffee table and a candle. I look around to see I'm still alone. Maybe he went to take a shower? If so, he'll be gone for a bit.

I check again, but nothing.

I light the candle and check one last time.

Nothing.

I slowly let the flame lick at my fingers, feeling no pain. After swirling my finger around in the flame, I lift gently like I'm picking up the most delicate butterfly. The flames follow, wrapping around my hand. This time, I focus on controlling the fire, making it do a seductive dance on my fingertips. I focus on keeping it from traveling down my arm.

It obeys.

"So, it's real."

The voice from behind me makes me nearly jump out of my skin. I whip around, using my other hand to extinguish the flame.

"Hey," I say, breathy. "I was just.. uh.."

There was a long pause while I ran through what I could possibly have been doing that would look remotely like controlling fire.

"You don't have a good excuse, do you?" Colson says with a chuckle.

"No," I say, defeated.

He looks down at my hand. I didn't realize how close he was standing. I can smell him. Expensive cologne, pine, with a hint of iron. He changed into grey sweatpants and a black hoodie. Curse those grey sweatpants—every straight girl's weakness.

He takes my hand, lifting it closer to his face and examining it. I stare at his dark eyes, watching them move back and forth, up and down. He flips my hand over and examines the other side. There are no burns or scars, in fact, my hand is warm and clammy. His eyes meet mine, sending a shiver in my gut. My heart is beating faster than it was when I was fighting for my life, not even an hour earlier.

He huffs, then releases my hand, not saying a word about what he just walked in on me doing. He grabs the food on the kitchen counter and brings it to the coffee table.

"Sit. Eat." He demands, dropping the food down.

I stand for a moment, not obeying his orders. He pulls a large blanket out of the closet to the side of the living room and brings it back to me. He sits in the center of the couch, fanning out the blanket so it's enough for both of us.

No. This isn't happening. I'm still mad.

I reach down and rip the whole blanket off of him, then tuck myself in the corner of the couch, trying my best to keep my distance.

He huffs out a chuckle before reaching for food.

"Feel better?" He asks, taking a bite of orange chicken.

"I'd feel better if I was at home." I scoff.

He drops his take-out container on the table and scoffs it back.

"Gee, thanks, *Colson*. I owe you! You saved my life from that deranged killer who would have gutted me." He says in a voice mocking me. "Any time, Codi, it was no problem. Just call me Superman, you know?" Switching back to his normal voice.

Blink. Blink.

I stare at him silently for a moment before realizing he has a point.

"Thank you," I whisper.

"What was that?" He mocks, throwing his hand up by his ear.

"Thank you, Colson!" I shout.

"Oh yeah, you're welcome." He says with a smirk.

I check my phone to see its after midnight. The TV turning on distracts me from the time.

"Is there anything you would like to watch?"

I stare at the remote he has extended out to me.

"Nothing in particular. You pick." My voice came out slightly hoarse.

He browses through the selection before picking a random rom-com.

I watch him for a moment, examining his features. The light reflects off his dark eyes. His lips, full and pink, surround the darkness of his stubble. It's the first time I notice his ears, slightly deformed from his fighting days.

"What?" His voice is deep.

"Are we not going to talk about it?" I say shyly.

"Talk about what?"

"What you walked in on me doing."

His lips pucker before turning to me to respond.

"Only if you want to talk about it." He smiles.

I look down at my hands, breaking eye contact.

"I don't know how to talk about it," I whisper.

"Then we don't have to talk about it." He says, turning back to the TV.

Silence falls on us again.

"So, we're just going to eat food and watch movies now?"

"Yup." His lips pop with the word.

I let a huff escape my nose as I looked back to the TV. Either he doesn't want to talk about it, or he thinks I don't want to talk about it. Either way, we're just going to pretend I wasn't nearly kidnapped, he came to my rescue after supposedly following me. He didn't just walk in on me with a handful of fire or that I'm sitting on his couch in his clothes. Since I will be here all night, I decided to make myself comfortable. I curl up in a ball, hugging the blanket tight. It smells like him. A dark green, soft, oversized blanket. It's incredibly comforting after tonight. I try my best to get comfortable, but something is missing.

I huff.

Colson glances at me, then gets up and leaves the room. Was I annoying him? Was this his only blanket down here? Did he decide to go to bed?

A few moments later, he comes back. I look up at him just as a pillow hits my face. I look at the pillow and then at him, not saying a word. I fluff up the pillow and lay it down.

That is precisely what was missing. How did he know? I'm starting to think this guy not only stalks me but can read my mind.

If you can read my mind, say "Twinkie".

Nothing. Okay, that's not it. Maybe it was a lucky guess. I lay my head down on the cloud of a pillow, relaxing my body for the night.

"Thank you," I whisper.

He leans over and pats my leg instead of saying anything, letting me know he heard me. I stare at the TV, clearing my head. My eyes begin to get heavy. I let them slowly close, occasionally hearing Colson let out a chuckle. All the energy and adrenaline of tonight wear off quickly while all the sounds of life fade away, sending me into a deep sleep.

CHAPTER

10

I wake up to the sound of the rain hitting the windows throughout the house. I was curled up, still in the blanket on the couch, my legs stiff from being curled up in a ball all night. I try to wipe the sleepiness off my face as I process my surroundings. I had that moment of panic, not realizing where I was before I finally remembered. I look over to see Colson fast asleep on the other side of the couch. I guess he's seriously taking the whole 'never letting me out of his sight' thing. That, or he just fell asleep while the movie was still running.

The TV is off now. The house is still, and the rain is the only noise. I can't even hear Colson breathing. He's so quiet.

I slowly make my way up, trying not to wake him. I manage to sneak into the downstairs bathroom.

Oh, god. I look like shit.

My hair is standing straight up on the side I was asleep on, my skin is pale, and I can tell already that my morning breath smells like death. I dig around the drawers and luckily find an old bottle of mouthwash. One problem was fixed. I throw water on my face and hair, attempting to tame it. After peeing, I head back out to the kitchen.

I look to the couch to see if Colson is still lying there.

"Good morning, love." He says in a deep, sleepy voice. It catches me off guard enough that I jump a little.

"Good morning," I grunt.

I sit down at the island and watch him. He's already made a fresh pot of coffee and now has fixings for breakfast laid out. He pulls out two mugs, fills each with coffee, adds creamer, and then slides one down the island to me.

"Thank you."

The coffee is at a reasonable temperature, with a splash of French vanilla creamer.

"Hungry?" He asks before sipping his coffee.

I nod. "I could eat."

Several minutes go by of silence as he begins making breakfast. Surprisingly, this isn't awkward at all. I figured sleeping at his house and about to have breakfast with him would be weird, but it feels... normal. Like we have known each other for our whole lives. But I don't even know how old he is. I never thought to ask. Getting up to detective level takes a long time, but he still looks so young. I would have to guess in the late twenties. Watching him, I realize he took his hoodie off and has a t-shirt on with his grey sweatpants.

"When is your next shift?" He asks, bringing me back to the room and out of my thoughts.

"Tomorrow," I say, clearing my throat.

He huffs and nods.

"You're taking me home today, right?"

He turns to look back at me with one brow raised.

"Yeah."

I sigh with relief when he says something else.

"I'll take you home to pick up some things, then bring you back here."

I whip my head up, brows pushed together.

"Colson."

"Codi." He says my name without even looking back at me.

"I can't stay here."

He only shrugs his shoulders, causing a bit of anger to build up in me.

"Colson!"

He finally turns to me, leaning back against the counter with his coffee in hand, looking almost amused.

"Colson, I have to go home. I can't stay here."

"Well, you're going to."

This has to be some form of kidnapping. He can't make me stay here. I spend several moments staring at him in disbelief.

"No," I say firmly.

"Yes." He matches my tone.

"This isn't a 'No means try harder' situation. I can't stay here. I have work."

"I'll take you too and from work."

"Oh, hell no!" I shout.

He looks at me, confused, waiting for me to explain.

"If the guys see me showing up and leaving with you, I'll never hear the end of it. And if they find out I've stayed the night here, god knows what they'll do."

He scoffs. "That's what you're worried about?"

I roll my eyes.

"You're so worried about what other people think that you're not even thinking about your safety. Codi, you were almost taken. And if I didn't show up when I did, you could be dead right now. I don't know if that guy knows where you live, so I'm not taking the chances. Please stay here where I can keep an eye on you. And if the guys at the firehouse want to taunt either of us about that, let them. It's better to be teased than dead."

I take a deep breath, but I have nothing to say back. He turns back around to continue working on breakfast. He has a point. I acted like I had everything under control and my one punch would make a difference. But in reality, that man was bigger and stronger than me. Hardly anyone was on the streets, and all the shops were closed. He could have grabbed me and taken off with me, and no one would have seen. I rest my forehead in my hand as I process everything.

"Fine," I whisper.

I don't have an argument anymore. All I want is to sleep in my own home, but the murderer could know where I live and still target me since I got away.

Colson fixes me a plate of scrambled eggs, bacon, and potatoes before sliding it over to me. After fixing himself a plate, he joins me at the island. I glance at the stove clock to see it's 6:25 am. No wonder I'm still so tired.

We sit in silence, eating, for several minutes when movement from Colson catches my eye. He gets up and walks to the living room, grabbing something off the coffee table. I watch him, sipping on my coffee, as he makes his way back to me. He walks so gracefully, hardly making noise. His muscular body glides with ease. He sits in his chair and places the candle from last night before me. I stare as he takes the lighter and lights the candle. Not saying a word, he puts down the lighter and continues eating. My eyes shift from the candle to him multiple times. He brings his eyes to mine, and we lift our brows simultaneously, both for a different question.

"Just setting the mood." He muffles with a mouth full of food.

My brows push together, and he smirks at my expression.

I lean forward and blow out the handle, watching the smoke of the wick rise. Colson looks at me, confused, then back to the candle. Without looking back up, he lights the candle.

Annoyed, I blow it out again, returning to my coffee.

This time, Colson holds eye contact with me as he lights the candle again and sets it down. I slam my hands down on the counter, push myself off the chair, and blow as hard as I can. But, this time, it doesn't go out. With all the anger built up in me, flames shot out of the candle, going in the direction I was blowing like I was a dragon or something. Startled, I slam myself back in the chair and notice some papers now on fire.

"Shit!" Colson huffs, jumping up to find something to extinguish the flames.

He finally puts it out with a damp towel and then looks at me. I don't think I have ever had my eyes so wide. I sit, just staring at the now burnt-to-a-crisp paper. I can feel Colson's eyes fixed on me.

"Well." He finally says. "I didn't expect that."

In a heartbeat, I jump up from my chair and start down the hall. Going where? I wasn't sure yet. I hear Colson calling my name from behind, but I keep walking. Halfway up the stairs, I turn back to see Colson standing at the bottom.

"You're taking me home today. I'm not staying here."

He opens his mouth to respond, but I cut him off.

"No arguments! If you're worried about my safety, assign someone to park outside my building, but I'm not staying here."

I give him the sternest look I can muster, as if my RBF isn't stern enough.

His face drops slightly. "Okay." He says in a hushed tone.

Victory. I win.

The drive back to my place was silent. The only sounds were the engine and the rain hitting the windshield. I watched the trees pass by in a flash, avoiding any conversation with Colson. He seemed to understand and didn't even try to talk about what happened this morning.

We pull up to the front door of my building. Colson throws the truck in park and takes his seatbelt off.

"What are you doing?" I ask nervously.

He looks at me, confused for a moment, before answering.

"I was going to go make sure your apartment was clear."

"You think this random guy from last night knows exactly where I live and was able to get into my home without anyone noticing? I think it's fine."

"Codi." He says firmly. "Just give me this peace of mind. Please."

I sigh but allow him to follow me inside.

He thoroughly checked my apartment and found it empty, everything in the same spot I left it the night before.

CHAPTER

11

The past few weeks have been exactly what I expected regarding work. Multiple lift assists, a few drug overdoses, sick and injured, a car wreck, and someone starting an oil fire in their kitchen—very little excitement. The most exciting part was having Cas teach me to play poker. I still don't understand it, nor am I any good. Snow has made its way to Clearwater, making my walks to and from work miserable. On the bright side, the cold helps me wake up first thing in the morning. It has also made getting to calls a much longer process. The snow has a layer of ice underneath it, making it mandatory to put chains on the medic rig and engine. So, 25mph is our max when getting anywhere.

I've gotten daily update requests from Colson.

Is everything okay? Have you seen that guy again? Did you make it home safe?

After so many times of me telling him everything was fine, I got annoyed enough to stop messaging him back. I chose to spend most of my time in the weight room at the station for a shift if I wasn't watching the worst movies possible with the guys. The sun set a while ago, but there was still a blueish glow outside with the thick, fluffy snow. The lights outside made the top layer sparkle like a million little stars on the ground. It's a beautiful view as I hit my tenth mile on the treadmill—droplets of sweat rain down my face. I have to keep wiping them away so they don't get in my eyes. My short hair, now hanging down past my ears, is drenched. My tablet, set perfectly in front of me, played my favorite show I'd already watched four times. But it's distracting me from my muscles, barking with each step.

A loud bang comes from my right side. I turn to see Colson swing open the door. Anger was plastered on his face.

"Are you fucking kidding me?" He shouts.

I guess the whole 'not responding' thing pissed him off. It had been almost 48 hours since his last message. I had my phone on vibrate all day and could feel it going off. So much so that I just left it in my bunk the whole shift.

I hop up to place my feet on each side of the treadmill as I bring it to a stop, also pausing my show. I turn to him, panting, one eyebrow raised, acting confused.

"Don't look at me like that." He growls.

"Like what?"

He huffs a laugh. "Like you don't know why I'm upset."

I roll my eyes and rest my arms along the treadmill panel.

"What do you want, Colson?" I scoff.

"You haven't messaged me back in two days. I had to track you down to ensure you were still alive."

"Obviously, I'm fine," I say, taking a step off with a towel and going to the bench along the wall. I grab my water bottle and pour water into my mouth, allowing it to miss and fall down my neck to cool me off. Refreshing.

"How was I supposed to know that? You wouldn't answer your phone, so I immediately thought the worst."

Colson started as a charming, caring guy, but now he's acting a little too controlling for comfort.

"What do you want from me, Colson? An update every minute? *Hey, I just woke up. I just got a cup of coffee. It was hot. Just stretched, back popped. Leo said hi to me this morning. Oh, I just passed some gas, I thought you'd like to know.* Is that what you want? Do you want to know what I'm doing at all times?

Because last time I checked, we're not dating. Therefore, you don't need to know what's happening at all times."

I took my towel and vigorously rubbed my hair with it, making it even more of a mess.

"Oh shit, my bad. Was I supposed to tell you I rubbed the sweat out of my hair, too? Sorry, forgot."

I stand up and start going out the door when my arm is grabbed, stopping me. I look down at the hand holding on to me, then glare at Colson.

"There's been two more murders." He whispers.

My face drops from anger to remorse for those poor girls.

"I know," I say softly.

Colson's eyes meet mine.

"It was on the news. Last shift got called to one of them too, so we got to hear details this morning at shift change."

his grip loosens to a light caress.

"One kind of looked like you. I got scared."

He was right. One of the girls looked similar to me. Same color hair, same body type, and skin tone. Her face was so mangled no one could Identify her right away. So, I don't blame him much for thinking it could have been me. Her body was so dirty, bruised, and bloody you couldn't tell if she had any tattoos either. His expression went from angry to sad. Sad for those girls, their families, and their friends.

"I know," I whisper.

His grip was still tight on my arm as my eyes tracked back up to his.

"I'm okay." My tone is soft and comforting. "If I'm not locked away at home, I'm here. You know damn well the guys would never let anything happen to me while they're around."

His grip loosens. "I'm sorry."

Before I could say a response, the tones went off.

"Station 31, respond to an attempted kidnapping at 275 Washoe Street."

275 Washoe Street. "Isn't that the old abandoned logging mill outside of town?"

A muscle in Colson's jaw flexes with the question.

"Dovetch! Let's go! You're on the medic unit for this one." Cap shouts out to me. "And Colson, you're probably gonna want to follow us up on this one."

I give Cap a quick nod and spring for my turn-out bottoms, sitting between the med unit and the engine. I bring the towel with me to continue drying my hair.

The snow was thicker the farther outside of town we got. The ambulance was rough, with the chains digging into the ice underneath. The ambulance and engine lights lit the snow in beautiful reds and whites, lighting up the trees extending from the fluffy snow. I prepped myself in the back, putting on the most miniature gloves the department supplies. Leo was kind enough to grab the department jacket I had lying on a chair in the dining room on his way out. At least the coat will cover my sweat smell. Austin tosses a beanie back at me.

"It's fucking freezing out there, Code. Stay warm." He shouts back.

As we pull up to the location, there are tons of cops and flashing lights lighting up the old, broken-down building. We stopped next to a patrol car, where I saw the girl sitting in the back seat covered in a blanket.

I grab the med bag sitting in its place next to the side door, then jump out. The cold air hits my face like a freight train, stinging my nostrils with every breath. I carefully make my way to the side the girl is on.

"She's real shaken up. It's probably a good idea if the female medic takes care of her. She's real jumpy with men." The officer next to the door informs Cap.

"Alright, Dovetch. Do your thing." Cap says, gesturing to the car door.

I push my way through the guys to get to the girl. The cold bites into my hand as I reach for the door handle.

The girl jumps and looks at me frantically as I open the door.

"It's okay," I say calmly. "My name is Codi. I'm here to take care of you."

She looks at me, scared and confused.

"Codi?" She whispers.

I nod.

"That.. isn't... isn't that a boy's name?" She stutters.

I let out a huff as I kneel to her level.

"Uh, yeah. My dad wanted all boys, then I came along."

She's shivering when I notice she has nothing on underneath the blanket. Her lip is cracked open, her left eye Is purple and black tone and bloodshot, a trail of dried blood clings to her upper lip, and there's a large laceration on her clavicle. I look down at her hands, gripping the life out of the blanket. Dirt and dried blood was bedded deep under her nails.

"Is it okay if I take you to the ambulance and check you out?" I make my voice higher pitched and soft. It was a motherly tone, hoping it would comfort her a bit.

She nods.

I look down at the cold snow I can feel through the knees of my turn-outs and then up to the guys. There are only men here. If she really was attacked and scared of men now, there was no way she was going to want one of them to carry her, no matter how good of a man they were. She's already shivering so much that I would hate to make her walk twenty feet to the ambulance and wait for them to open the doors. Colson made it and is now standing a little ways behind me. I meet his eyes as he stares at the poor girl before me.

I grab my med bag and hold it out for someone to take. Everyone looks at me, slightly confused, probably thinking I would ask them to take her.

"Put your arm around my neck, okay?"

She hesitates halfway but does as I ask. I bring myself to a squat position, bringing one arm around her back and the other under her legs, ensuring the blanket covers where my ice cube hands touch. Using my leg strength, I pull her closer to my body and lift her out of the patrol car. She clings to me.

I turn slightly to see every pair of eyebrows raised.

Yeah. I've been working out. What about it?

The snow crunched under my boots with every step to the ambulance. Cap rushes over and swings the back door open so I can step up and lay the girl on the gurney. As I release her, I follow her eyes, staring out the door, frightened. I see movement from a broken window on the second floor. It's too big to be any animal hiding out there. I jump up and slam my hand on the door as Colson attempts to close it, making a loud thud.

"Did they clear the building?"

Colson raises a brow before answering.

"They did."

My eyes travel back to the window.

"Check again." My tone was more demanding than I expected, and by the look on Colson's face, more than he expected as well. He nodded and shouted at the officers to clear the building again. Most of them rolled their eyes, simply wanting to go home and escape the cold, but they obeyed.

On the way to the hospital, my hand never left the grasp of the girls. She's 23, and she just moved here a few months ago. Her name is Amber. Her long black hair clings to her face, coated in blood and melted snow. The guys work on getting her vitals, and I comfort her the whole way. Cap calls the hospital once we are a few minutes out to notify them so they can prep.

Colson pulls up minutes after we get the girl out, my hand still intertwined in hers. She only releases when a female nurse takes my place.

"Thank you, Codi." Amber's raspy voice calls out to me.

"You're welcome," I say softly, watching her be wheeled away to a room.

Colson makes his way to my side.

"Get any info?" He asks.

"Not anything useful. Just that he was wearing a mask and all black."

He nods. "I'll ask her a few questions once she's settled."

He begins to walk away when I grab his arm above his elbow, halting him.

He raises a brow, surprised but silently waiting.

"Anything?" I whisper.

His expression relaxes.

"No." He breathes. "Obvious evidence someone was there but no sign of the suspect. We'll keep looking."

He caresses my hand holding his arm before walking away and disappearing into the room Amber was taken into.

CHAPTER

12

The seasons have begun to change, and the weather is getting warmer but still cold enough to need a light jacket outside. The murders have stopped since we found Amber. We're all hoping they finally stopped completely, but Colson says otherwise.

"He got scared because we almost caught him. He's laying low for a while." He would say when we talked at the station.

The department banquet is this Friday. I thought we would wear our uniforms, but everyone says they wear black ties. I don't own a formal dress. I have a few sun dresses for family occasions, but nothing fancy. So, I decided to spend my day off doing a little shopping to see if I could find something.

My black leggings fit snugly to my legs as I walk down Main Street past all the little shops, my jacket zipped up to my neck, and my white tennis shoes.

I had stopped in a few shops only to find some candles and a few random things to put around the apartment. I heard my name from ahead as I slowly walked down the street.

"Codi!" A girl shouts out.

I met Sarah, Leo's girlfriend, whom I've met a few times when she stopped by to drop off food for us.

Her long, silky blond hair sways in the wind as she skips towards me. Her oversized hoodie, I'm assuming, is Leo's, and ripped jeans paired with a pair of sandals. Leo did well finding this one. She is the definition of 'her smile lights up a room.' Golden skin, sun-kissed even in the dark months. Her bright blue eyes meet mine, and her big, white smile grows as she gets closer.

I allow a smile to grow on my face for her. I do not usually want to hang out with friends, but Sarah is always a joy. Her bubbly energy helps brighten anyone's mood.

She embraces me in a hug, and her vanilla-scented perfume engulfs my senses.

"What brings you out today?" She asks cheerfully.

"Day off," I reply. "Decided to take some time to find a dress for the banquet."

She glances down at my bags and then back to me.

"Did you find one?"

"I haven't."

Her big smile grows on her face again.

"Want some company? Leo is busy for a few hours, so I have time to kill."

As much as I enjoy my peace, I take her up on that offer. Having another girl's opinion on dresses may help.

She locked arms with me, and we continued where I was heading.

"I passed the cutest dress shop about a block from here. I think you'll find something beautiful there." Her voice is continuously cheerful.

I don't think this girl could ever sound angry. Her energy is just a bright, warm light that embraces anyone she comes in contact with.

We make it to the shop, and she opens the door for me. Walking in, it smells like vanilla beans and roses, and pop music plays lightly throughout the store.

"Welcome in!" a woman with shoulder-length jet-black hair says from behind the counter. "Is there Anything I can help you guys find?" she asks politely.

"We are on the lookout for some beautiful yet sexy dresses for a fire department banquet. This girl needs to walk in the room and have every head turn to her." Sarah says, shaking my arm, which is still locked in hers.

I let out a chuckle. "Just a simple, black dress is fine."

Sarah gasps. "Simple? No way. You need to make every jaw in the room drop, girl. You are beautiful! Flaunt it!"

I expected that, working with all men, I would threaten their girlfriends, as I'm the only female they work with. But Sarah has been nothing but kind to me.

We spend almost an hour looking and trying on dresses together.

"Hey, Leo just texted me. He's going to be a little longer. His mom needs help with some things." Sarah's voice comes from the dressing room beside me. "I was thinking about getting a spray tan if you'd want to come with."

A spray tan probably wouldn't hurt. My skin has gotten so pale in the winter months.

"As long as we can get some lunch first. I'm starving."

"Okay!" She cheers.

After hanging around guys for so long, having a girl's day might be good.

Every dress I tried did not feel right, so I put on the last one I had picked.

"None of these feel right," I mumble. Apparently, it was loud enough for Sarah to hear.

Her curtain flies open.

"Come out so I can see."

I swing my curtain open to see her in an adorable black silk dress, her bare feet on the carpet.

I wore a black spaghetti-strap ball gown with way too much poof.

"I feel like I'm wearing a gothic wedding gown."

Sarah's face scrunches as she examines me.

"I wish I could disagree, but it does look like that. Go back in, and I'll go find something for you." She says, spinning around, her dress flowing with every movement as she disappears into the display of dresses.

I hide in the dressing room, remove the gothic wedding dress, and wait. A few moments later, a dress is shoved through the curtain's opening.

"Try this one! I think it's your size."

The blood-red silk is soft to the touch. It feels thin and light. It glides onto my body with ease, like it was specifically made for my body type. It hugs my curves in all the right places. The spaghetti straps were thin lines across my muscular shoulders, complementing them. The built-in bralette lifts my breasts just enough for them to be more noticeable. The tattoo on my right leg sits exposed by the hip-high slit in the dress. I twist around to see the back of the dress so low it reveals the two little dimples on the lowest part of my back. Any lower, and my ass would be hanging out. But it feels so good. I've been wearing my uniform, jeans, or sweats for so long that I almost forgot how toned my whole body has become.

"Does it fit?" Sarah calls out from behind the curtain.

"Like a glove," I mumble back.

The curtain rips open, and Sarah's jaw nearly hits the floor.

"Girl." She breathes. "You have to wear that to the banquet."

"You don't think it's a little," I glance at myself in the mirror again. "Exposing?"

"I mean." She crosses her arms and examines me. "If Leo stares for too long, I'll slap him, but you are jaw-droppingly gorgeous. I couldn't blame him. I might stare for a while, too." She laughs.

I huff a breath, glaring back to her with a small smile growing.

"Colson is going to love this."

I whirl around at his name.

"Colson?"

She cocks her head to one side, confused as to why I'm confused.

"Colson Delose." She says almost a question. "Leo said you two were, like, a thing."

I roll my eyes, turning back to the mirror.

"We are definitely not a thing. He's been keeping me updated on the murders and everything since I've gotten a lot of calls involving them. So, if I notice anything at the scene or the victim tells me, I let him know. He also spends way too much time at the station."

One shoulder lifts as she smirks at me.

"Whatever you say."

I glare at her for a moment.

"You have to admit. He's super hot. Don't tell Leo I said that." She chuckles.

"Trust me, I won't. I will punch him for saying that Colson and I are a thing, though."

She shrugs again.

"He probably deserves it."

CHAPTER

13

I stand in front of my full-body mirror, staring at the person looking back at me. My jaw-length hair is slightly curled to frame my face, my calves pop out with the position my heels put me in, and the tattoos lining my arms and right leg see the light for the first time in months. I managed to do a full face of makeup, accompanied by false lashes and all. My lips are painted red to match the silky dress that contours my every curve.

God, this dress.

I can't tell if it's too much or just enough. It will definitely remind the fire guys that I am indeed a female.

A knock comes from the front door beside me. I pat my hands on my dress to flatten stray wrinkles before opening the door.

"Ay, your Uber is here. I charge by the second with a $20 down payment and-" Austin's eyes widen as he looks me over, his eyebrows nearly reaching his hairline.

"Whoa." He breathes.

"Thanks for picking me up. I appreciate the ride."

I turn back to grab my jacket and purse lying on the kitchen island, my heels clicking with every step. I turn back to see Austin still staring with wide eyes.

"What?" I ask, completely oblivious.

"You look," he looks me up and down again. "Beautiful."

His voice was rough on the last word.

I can't control the smile growing on my face while my cheeks flush.

"Thank you." I nod.

He blinks. "You ready?"

I nod again, starting to the door.

I glance at Austin as I lock the door to my apartment. His tux is tailored perfectly to his muscular body.

"You look very handsome," I say, keeping pace beside him.

I could have sworn I saw him blush.

The drive was short. Austin blasted music the whole way, singing along like he was serenading me. We pulled into a parking spot at the hotel where the banquet was being held. Austin rushes to my side and opens my door, holding a hand for me.

"Such a gentlemen." I tease.

We lock arms as we walk in through the doors, following the signs to the ballroom. Everyone is in beautiful dresses and suits, except for the few battalion chiefs and captains in their dress uniforms.

"Holy Hell!" A voice calls out from the table to our right.

I look over to see Cas, Leo, and Eddie all staring in our direction.

"Codi is a girl?" Eddie teases.

I curtsy to them, being a little more awkward than I anticipated. Sarah sits next to Leo with a big smile, knowing damn well this is her doing. I sit on the other side of Sarah and begin our casual conversation. I sip on my fruity mixed drink when the empty chair beside me scoots back.

"Sorry, I'm late. Had a few things to finish up at the station."

I nearly choke on my drink as Colson sits down. I was wondering why Austin didn't take that seat and sat in the one next to Cas. I just figured he wanted to talk to him more than listen to me and Sarah babble on about girly things. I also didn't know he would even be here. I thought this was only for firefighters and their families.

"There's my plus one!" Austin calls out, slapping Colson's hand, turning it into a handshake.

Colson is the only guy at the table who isn't wearing a tie, but his suit is clean and tailored, fitting perfectly to his toned muscles.

Fuck, he looks good.

"You made Colson your plus one?" I ask Austin.

"Fuck yeah, I did." He says, slapping Colson's shoulder. "My big handsome detective."

"Gag," Sarah says next to me. "Get a room, you two."

"We are in a hotel. Maybe they'll give us the honeymoon suite."

The guys all laugh at Austin's comment. I use almost every muscle to not gawk at Colson next to me. Fighting every urge to stare at his biceps, pushing the limits of his selves as he reaches for his drink. As the guys carry on their conversation, I feel heat come from my side.

"You look beautiful," Colson whispers in my ear.

My whole body tingles as his breath hits my ear, flowing down my neck. Every hair on the back of my neck stood straight up with the soft yet rough whisper.

God damn it, Codi. Pull yourself together. Say something confident so he doesn't know he is affecting you like this.

"So I've been told," I whisper back, bringing my eyes to his, realizing how close we are now. The corner of his mouth elevates as he looks from my eyes to my lips and then back to my eyes.

Fuck.

He pulls away first, sitting back up straight. Trying to act like nothing happened, I sip my drink.

The award ceremony lasted much longer than we had hoped, but we all stood and cheered as Caption Kelso got the "Caption of the Year" award. We were definitely the most obnoxious table there, but it got Cap to smile our way while accepting the award. Once all the awards were handed out, they opened the empty part of the floor for everyone to dance. As soon as the lights go down and the music starts blasting, Austin, Cas, and Eddie all gang up on me to get me onto the dance floor.

I managed to dance a few songs with the guys without twisting my ankle in these heels. Austin grabs me, pulling me closer to him to dance.

"Having fun?" He asks with a smile.

"I am, actually," I say, returning the smile.

"Oh good." He cheers, sending me spinning around until I'm slammed against someone else.

"You should wear a dress more often, code. You look nice," Eddie says, wrapping his arms around me as I stumble.

"Thank you. You look very handsome tonight."

Before Eddie could respond, my right elbow was tugged, pulling me into Cas's arms.

Ok, I'm starting to get dizzy.

"I really believe you should have won Rookie of the Year with the amount of saves you had."

"Better luck next year, I guess." I laugh before I'm spun around again, slamming into Leo this time.

He takes my hand and pulls me closer to dance.

"Hey, you." I cheer.

He responds with a smile. He's so much taller than me. I barely reach his collarbone.

"So, why have you been telling your girlfriend that Colson and I are dating?"

He smirks and shrugs his shoulders.

"You guys make a cute couple. What can I say?"

"Yeah, not happening." I cough.

I see his eyes drift up behind me.

"We'll see." He says, sending me into a spin across the floor.

I slam into another body as the tempo of the music slows down. I look up to meet Colson's dark brown eyes. I look around to see everyone split off into couples to slow dance. The lights dim down to add to the mood. A mood that I don't want at this moment. The blue-tented lights shaded his face, reflecting off his midnight-black hair. The white button-up shirt under his suit jacket was unbuttoned just enough to show off a sneak peek of his toned chest. The feral part of me craved to see the rest of him.

"Hi." He said softly, looking down at me. "May I have this dance?"

I hesitate before nodding and taking the hand he has extended out. He pulls me in and rests his other hand on the curve of my lower back, which my dress exposes. Shock travels up my spine, engaging every muscle in my back to keep me from shuttering at his touch. I glance over to Sarah, now dancing closely to Leo. She meets my eyes, smiles, and gives a thumbs-up in my direction.

Shaking my head, I bring my eyes back to Colson, who is already looking down at me. My heart stutters when our eyes meet.

"So, uh." I try to converse, hoping this feeling will stop twisting in my gut. "Did you hear that the guys are telling people we're a thing?"

Smooth.

Colson huffs a laugh and looks to Austin and Eddie, who are now slowly dancing with each other, touching a little more than anyone else.

"That doesn't surprise me. They thrive on gossip."

I let a small chuckle escape as awkward silence overcomes us.

"So," Colson says, breaking the silence. "Been practicing?"

I furor my brow at him.

"The fire-bending stuff." He explains.

I shush him a little louder than I expected, looking around to see if anyone heard.

"You're trying to keep it a secret?"

I shrug my shoulder in response.

"I don't know how people would react," I murmur.

He nods understandably.

"Am I the only one who knows?" He whispers.

I meet his dark eyes and nod.

"How can I help?"

His question sounds sincere, warming my cheeks. I shake my head, not knowing how he even could. Neither of us knows how to explain this, let alone control it. I've learned to control some of it, but still not enough to use it as a party trick any time soon.

"Just know I'm always here to help. Whatever I can do to figure this out with you."

He whispers, leaning closer to my face. The short distance between us twists my gut. My eyes betray me, glancing down at his lips and then back to his eyes, only to find his doing the same.

The song finally ends, turning back into a dance beat. My mouth opens slightly with a shallow breath.

"I should probably see if Austin will take me home. I'm getting tired." I say, backing away a step.

We both turn to see Austin and Eddie dancing like wild animals on the side of the dance floor. Austin looks like he's having too much fun to interrupt now.

"I can take you home. He seems to be preoccupied."

I can't argue that. I know I wouldn't hear the end of how I'm such a party pooper. But on the other hand, I won't hear the end of how I slow danced with Colson, then left with him. I can't tell which will be more annoying. I could always text him and say I got a ride. I'm not saying from whom, but I'm sure they'll see Colson is gone and put two and two together.

"I'll go talk to him. See what he wants to do before deciding."

Perfect, I'll ask him if he wants to leave. That way, if he says yes, I'm not a party pooper. If he says no, it won't look like I wanted to leave with Colson in the first place.

I make my way over to the guys, heels clicking on the hardwood floor. I grab Austin's arm and gently tug. He whips around to see me, acts excited, then throws an arm over my shoulders.

"I'm ready to go. Do you want to stay or head out?"

I shout over the music, praying he wants to go home, too.

"Leave? Already? The party just started!" He shouts back.

I guess he wants to stay.

"I can get another ride if you want to stay. It's no big deal."

"No!" He pouts. "Stay with us! Have some fun."

He wraps me up in a hug, and I can smell the alcohol on him. He's been drinking. I guess that's my answer right there.

"You've been drinking," I shout into his chest. "I'll just get a ride, okay?"

I pull away from his grasp to see his sad puppy dog eyes.

"I'll see you guys next shift," I say to Austin and Eddie. Eddie nods while Austin rolls his eyes.

"Fine." He grunts.

I return to Colson, grab my stuff, and let him drive me home.

CHAPTER

14

Jogging through downtown is a peaceful way to start the day. Noise-canceling headphones drown out the sounds of passing cars and people. I keep my hood up to conceal my face as sweat drips down my temples. The weather still can't decide whether to remain winter or change to spring.

I'm jolted out of my little world as my shoulder slams into another. I whip around, pulling my right earbud out to apologize when my eyes are met with a familiar pair looking back. His dark brown hair, slightly falling over his brows, now raised at the impact, complementing his golden skin. Bright blue eyes reflected every bit of light from the cloud-covered sun, a sharp jawline covered in dark stubble, and broad shoulders caressed with a black, zip-up, hooded jacket, barely exposing his numerous tattoos. The familiar smell of him brings a flood of emotions I had been locking behind a door for months.

"Trevor?" My voice cracks.

A smile grows on his face as he recognizes me.

"Holy shit, Codi!" He chirps like he's happy to see me.

"I thought you moved out of state? What are you doing here?"

"I was going to move, but by the time I got everything packed, it just didn't feel right leaving, you know? So I canceled everything, just moved houses instead."

Trevor and I broke up not long after I found out I was accepted into the academy. He had wanted us to move to Oregon, get a house, and start a new life together. I hadn't told him I applied to the department until I was accepted. It took a toll on our relationship when I told him I couldn't move with him. My career here was far more important than starting a new life elsewhere. I felt terrible for that, but, at the same time, it's what would truly make me happy. And if that meant not having him by my side through it, I was willing to take that chance. As selfish as that is, I needed to think of myself in that moment. Just like my mother, he didn't agree with that path. Any time I brought it up, he'd shut me down or tell me not to do it, and if I loved him, I wouldn't. It made me realize maybe I didn't love him as much as he loved me.

"Hey, are you busy? Would you like to grab a coffee with me and catch up?"

I nod.

The coffee shop wasn't as busy as I thought, but we got a table next to the window, letting the sun rays peek out behind clouds to warm us. I held the coffee cup between both my hands, enjoying the warmth it gave off.

"So, how have you been? Tell me everything?" His voice is far more cheerful than the last time we spoke.

"Well, I made it through the academy, got on at a department. I've been busy with that."

"Oh yeah, the 24-hour shifts and all."

I huff a laugh and nod.

"Yeah, those get challenging at times."

"I could imagine."

"It's been gratifying, though."

"I saw on the news that you got trapped in that apartment fire. Must have been scary."

My eyes drift down to my coffee, remembering the moments when I honestly thought I was going to die in that fire.

"Yeah, it was, but I made it out fine."

Silence falls over us for a moment.

"I miss you." He whispers.

I bring my eyes to him, sadness flooding those blue eyes.

"I miss you, too."

The words came out before I could think about it. Do I miss him? Or do I miss the happy moments we had? I spent the last few months of our relationship hiding things because I knew he would fight me on them. He would try and talk me out of going into the fire service, resulting in arguments. I had always dreamed of following in my father's footsteps, but I did not need someone who never supported me as a partner. It was hard enough having my own family not support me.

"I still love you." He wishers again.

The words made my spine tighten. I don't want to have this conversation with him. I lean back in my chair, trying to figure out what to say next.

"I miss you so much and think about you all the time. I think about how things could have been different."

"If I didn't go to the fire academy?" I ask, knowing the honest answer.

His eyes lock on mine.

"I mean, if we worked out."

I clear my throat. "Trevor, I–"

"I know, I know." He interrupts. "I didn't want you to have such a dangerous job. I mean, can you blame me? With what happened to your dad, that fire you got trapped in."

"Don't." This time, I interrupt. "What happened to my dad was a freak accident. It could have happened to anyone. That doesn't mean it will happen to me. Besides, I have an amazing crew that won't let anything happen to me. Those guys would risk their lives to save me in a heartbeat."

His eyes travel down to the table in front of us.

"I know."

More silence falls. My phone lights up next to me, displaying a text message.

Colson:
What are you doing today?

Codi:
I'm at the coffee shop downtown right now. Why?

Colson:
I'm coming to get you.

Codi:
Why?
Codi:
I'm with someone right now.
Codi:
Hello?
Read:12:34pm

"Something wrong?" Trevor asks, bringing my attention back to him.

I shake my head. "Just a friend who wants to meet up."

I guess that's a good way of getting out of this conversation. I don't want to have to explain to him repeatedly why we didn't work and why I can't come back. Even sitting down for coffee with him was a bad idea.

Luckily, the conversation didn't return to the previous topic. As I step outside, the sun peeking out from behind dark clouds blinds me momentarily.

"Look, Codi," Trevor says as he grips my arm.

I cringe slightly, remembering the attack not that long ago. Flashbacks of that rainy night run through my mind before snapping myself out of it.

"I'm sorry about how things ended with us. I'm sorry I wasn't supportive. I just wanted you safe."

And to be your housewife.

I shake the thought away before it slips out.

"Trevor, I…" I'm interrupted by a car horn—Colson's truck squeals to a stop beside us.

"Your friend?"

I sigh. "Yeah."

Colson rolls down the window wearing a grey T-shirt that fits snuggly on his body, exposing every muscle across his chest and arms. Black, square-rimmed glasses hide his brown eyes from the short-lived sun.

"Com'n Code." He says, leaning over to push the passenger door open for me.

I look back to Trevor and shrug. "I'm being summoned."

He huffs a laugh.

"I'll see you around, okay?"

Trevor glances down, then back to me.

"Yeah." He whispers.

I resist the urge to hug him goodbye, which may strengthen his feelings again, as I climb into Colson's truck, leaving him alone on the sidewalk while the rain begins again.

"Who was that?" Colson breaks the silence as Trevor disappears from view.

"No one." I sigh.

He was no one he needed to be concerned about. The only threat Trevor gives off is a threat to my emotional health, with how he has a way of making me feel bad about looking after myself or how everything that goes wrong is my fault. Even if he had changed, I wasn't ready to take that chance yet.

"Where are we going?" I ask, trying to change the subject before he pries any more.

"The gym."

My brows push together at the response.

"You're taking me to the gym?"

He nods.

I wait for an explanation, but It doesn't come.

We pull up to an old, run-down building, and I am surprised I've never gotten any calls. Any metal is rusted, wood rotting, and bricks chipped and crumbling. The old, rusted sign on the front of the building only reads "Gym." This place looks abandoned.

Colson throws the truck in park, slides out through the door, and opens the back door to grab a large duffle bag resting in the back seat. I watch him momentarily before returning to the old, run-down building. As I examine the building, my door swings open, startling me.

"Well." Colson waves his hand, gesturing for me to get out of the truck. "Let's go."

I narrow my eyes at him.

"Did you bring me here to kill me?"

He coughs a laugh. "Come on."

Making our way to the front door, I expect the inside to reflect the outside. But when Colson opens the door for me, I'm shocked.

Beautiful hardwood flooring pathways lead to cushioned mats where weights and machines sit under the warm lights. Thick punching bags hang from the lower parts of the ceiling, mirrors lining the walls. In the dead center of the building stands a boxing cage. The chains were clean and shining under the lights, the flooring spotless. There's no cobwebs, rust, or even dust. My jaw drops at how clean and organized this place is. A few men, covered in tattoos and sweat, use some bags and weights, and one uses a jump rope in the corner facing the mirror. Each man Is tall and lean, built similarly to Colson.

Colson's hand grazes my lower back, pushing me towards a bag to our right. My eyes don't stop scanning the beautiful gym. The thud of Colson's duffle bag hitting the floor brings my attention back to him.

"Here." He says, tossing me a pair of boxing gloves.

"We're here to box?"

Colson looks up from his bag as he pulls a roll of wraps out of a side pocket. A smile creeps on his face as the lights sparkle in his eyes.

"It is a boxing gym. That's kind of what you do here."

I scoff.

He waves his fingers so I can come closer to him. The gesture is dominant and wildly attractive.

"Come here. I'll wrap you up."

He takes my hand and begins wrapping it in a thin, black wrap around each finger and knuckle, his callused hand brushing against the smooth skin on my hand. He then moves on to the next hand.

"Why did you bring me here?"

Colson's eyes snap up to me.

"I'm going to teach you how to fight." He smiles.

"I know how to fight." I scoff.

He raises a brow at the comment.

"I do!"

"Okay, okay. Prove it then."

He pats the bag to my right, causing it to swing slightly.

I clear my throat and slip on the boxing gloves. I glance back at Colson as I stand before the swaying bag. I haven't boxed in years, but muscle memory takes over.

Right hook, left hook.

I look back to Colson, who nods in approval.

Right jab, left jab, right hook.

I shake out my wrists as they ache slightly from the impact.

Right jab, left jab, right jab, jab, left hook, right jab, left uppercut, hard right hook.

Each hit is more brutal than the last. The bag sways back and forth.

"Alright," Colson says, gripping the bag to stop it from swinging. "Feeling warmed up yet?"

I look back at him and huff a breath.

"Sure." I sigh.

Colson takes my arm and leads me to the cage, opening the door.

"In you go." He says as he slaps my ass, encouraging me to go inside.

I whip around and throw a punch in his direction. He dodges, laughing at my sad attempt.

"Save it for the ring." He laughs.

When did he get so ballsy? And pushy?

"Shoes off!" Colson shouts.

I face him, narrowing my brow as he points to my shoes. I glance down at my hands, tightly tucked away in my boxing gloves, then back to Colson. With as much attitude as I can muster up, I kick one shoe in his direction. He dodges right as it flies past his head, but just as he thinks he is safe, my next shoe flies through the air, smacking him right in the side of the head. He grunts.

I can't help but let a chuckle escape.

"Well, come on." I laugh. "We don't have all day."

He scoffs, then removes his shoes and puts them to the side. Grabbing some striking pads, he makes his way to me. He claps the pads together, the sound echoing through the gym. He brings one up.

Left jab.

"Good." The other pad goes up.

Right jab.

The pad goes up, then another.

Left jab, right hook.

"Alright," Colson says, amused.

Left jab, right jab, left hook, right jab.

We continue multiple combos, not missing a beat.

"Who taught you?"

"My dad. I also grew up with brothers. Whatever they did, I did too."

Jab, jab, jab.

The sound of someone dropping weights catches my attention, startling me. As I glance over to where the noise came from, my head is jolted to my chest as Colson hits my head with one of the pads.

"Hey!" I shout.

"Pay attention." He snaps, throwing the pads back up.

Jab, jab, right hook, jab.

He brings the pad down low, and, with everything in me, I bring my leg up, using my heel to slam into him, sending him stumbling back, nearly hitting the chains. He looks back at me, surprised.

"Okay." He chuckles.

I hear other laughs come from around the gym.

"Gloves off," Colson says, throwing his pads down to the side of the mat.

I give him a confused look as I force the gloves off my hands. He hops on each foot a few times before lunging for me. When a man of Colson's size is barreling towards me, an average person's fight or flight response will encourage them to run, but I allow him to grip me around the waist. Noticing his mistake right away, I send my right arm down to hook around his throat, grab onto my left hand, and slightly pull up, putting him in a guillotine lock. He falls to one knee, also bringing me down to a knee. A light choke comes from him as I pull up on his throat more. Two taps on my hip tell me he's done. I release immediately, throwing my hands up. He looks up to me, holding his throat. More chuckles come from beside us.

I raise a brow to Colson. He nods and lunges again, taking me to my back. I wrap my legs around his waist, locking my ankles together. He puts his weight on my body, making it slightly difficult to breathe, but I manage to bring myself to grip on to his lats bulging from his shirt. I hook one foot around his, throw my other to the floor for leverage, and force my body weight on him, twisting him over onto his back and slamming him to the mat. In a heartbeat, I have his wrist in my hand, swing my leg over his neck, pulling his arm close to my chest. I lightly thrust my hips into his arm, putting him in a tight arm bar. He slaps my leg twice again, tapping out.

"What the fuck?" He laughs.

Even more laughter erupts from around us. I looked up to find the few guys who had been working out and were now watching us closely.

"Looks like you met your match, Delose!" One of the guys shouts, gripping the chains.

I roll back, springing to my feet. Colson looks up at me from his back with total surprise and amusement.

"So, what was that about teaching me to fight?"

A smile grows on his face as he sighs.

"Okay, I get it. You know what you're doing, " he says, jumping to his feet. "Let's try a few more things."

Lock, tap. Lock, tap. Lock, tap.

I had multiple rounds with multiple victories in my favor before Colson finally decided to give up. We finally exit the cage. Colson sits on a bench, putting everything in its spot in his bag.

"What are you doing later tonight?" Colson asks, looking up through his sweat-soaked hair.

"I was planning on ordering takeout and watching movies."

"I'm taking you out." The words leave him so naturally.

My brows push together, confused.

"Why, Mr. Delose, are you taking me on a date?"

I make the question as much of a joke as possible. Part of me hopes that is not the case, but the feral woman on her throne in my mind is praying it is.

He coughs out a laugh as he zips up his bag.

"Consider it an educational night out."

He stands up, hauls the bag over his shoulder, wraps his arm around my shoulders, and leads me out of the gym.

CHAPTER

15

When Colson picks me up from my apartment, the rain comes down hard, and the windshield wipers barely keep up. I try to stay awake as we drive down the interstate, watching cars pass. After a long, hour-long drive, Colson pulls off the freeway and eventually into a parking lot of what looks like a small restaurant. I step out of the truck onto the gravel parking lot, noticing multiple couples approaching the door. A wooden sign stands next to the walkway as we approach the door.

Rita's presents:
Lana chance
Fire Dancer
_7 pm_
$20 per person at door.
_21+_

I look to Colson, who pulls out his wallet to pay the man at the door.

"Fire dancer?" I ask him as we make our way through the door.

"Yes, ma'am. I thought you might like this show."

The corners of his mouth curl into a smile.

The inside of the building is decorated in different tints of red cloth hanging from the ceiling, round tables surrounding a small ring in the middle set up like a stage, each with small red candles. The lights are dim but light enough to see where we are walking. We are led to a table off to the side by a woman dressed in all black with her hair pulled up into a ponytail that sways with every step. We sit in the cushioned chairs a few tables away from what I was guessing is the stage. More and more people file in and take their seats.

Colson orders us two beers, and they arrive faster than at any other restaurant I've ever been to. As the waitress quickly turns to walk away, the wind from her movement blows out our small, delicate candle. I raise my brows and then look to Colson, who has the same expression. A smile grows on his face, and we both chuckle. He goes to raise his hand to call the waitress back over when I lightly grab his arm.

"Hold on," I whisper, leaning closer to him.

His brows raise again, lowering his hand.

I glance around the room to see no one paying any attention to us. I pick up the little candle, bringing it between us. I lift my index finger and concentrate on calling on a single flame. A tiny spec of light starts on the tip of my finger, quickly turning into a single flame dancing over my skin. It twirls and flickers, doing its typical, seductive dance. Colson huffs, and I look at him and see him smiling at my finger. His dark eyes flicker with amazement as the light of my tiny flame reflects in them. I bring the flame to the wick and relight the candle. I look back to Colson as I whip my hand to extinguish the flame, letting a smile grow.

"That's so fucking cool," Colson whispers to me.

I laugh out my nose when something to my side catches my attention. I look to my right to see large, red curtains swaying like someone had just hidden behind them. I stare at the curtains momentarily before brushing the weird feeling off and bringing my attention to my drink.

"Ladies and gentlemen!" A man's voice calls out from all around us. I glance forward to see a man dressed in a classic red ring leader costume.

"Thank you all for joining us on this wonderful evening of magic, amazement, and wonder!" He continues. "I am very excited to introduce tonight's act. Born in Romania, she moved to the States at a young age to pursue the 'American Dream.' And tonight, you all are so lucky to witness her beautiful talent. Beautiful, hypnotic, sexy."

The last word was said with a growl.

"I present to you the fire tamer, Lana Chance!"

The crowd cheers, clapping and whistling as the lights dim down. As the man exits, a ring of fire ignites. As they dim, a stunning woman appears in the ring's center. She's wearing a long, red skirt, split up on both sides so each tan leg is exposed, an anklet on her left ankle, and a bright red bra with jewels and chains dangling from it. Her hair is a bright red, matching her clothes, and pulled up in a high ponytail with beads placed throughout. Her hands are tattooed with swirls and lines traveling up the fingers and then up her arm. Her lips matched her bright red outfit, and dark smokey eyeshadow came to a point on the corners of her eyes. She's hypnotizing, for sure. I can see the intensity of her arctic blue eyes from several feet away. She begins an intricate dance, flowing her arms through the air. The flames start to dance with her, swirling round and round. As she twirls around, the fire follows so gracefully. Soon, she faces us again, moving her hands in such magical ways, and then the flames grow, turning into little tornadoes spinning around her. They follow her every move until she raises her hands and causes a fire trail to shoot through the air, spinning around the room but not catching anything on fire on its way past. Minutes feel like hours as I watch the hypnotizing dance of flames circle in the air, changing shape and obeying the women's every command.

"Wow," I say with a breath.

I don't think I've ever been so mesmerized by fire, and I have seen fire do things. The flames shape into a dragon as they fly above us, twisting through the air. My eyes drift down to the woman who is already looking at me. Our eyes meet, and an intense chill runs down my spine. I can feel my smile fade as she stares deep into my eyes. She waves her hands around, and her dragon of flames twists around her, then charges right to us. A split second of panic fills my gut, and I wave my hands in front of me in a heartbeat, splitting the dragon in two before it has a chance to touch us. It splits off both sides as the heat hits me right in the face. The flames extinguish on the sides as the women and I stare at each other. My brows raised high in shock. She lifts her chin and then nods slightly at me.

My heart is now racing, and my knees buckle under me. I slap my hand on the table, catching myself before I fall. Colson's hand is quickly at my back.

"She did that on purpose," I whisper to Colson as I sit back in my chair.

"What do you mean?" He asks.

"She knows what I am. She knew I could do that."

I can feel Colson's confused gaze on me.

"Do you know her?"

I shake my head slowly as I watch her continue her performance.

As the show ends, I am still shocked at what happened. The crowd begins to murmur to themselves while some head for the door. I throw back the last of my drink when a large man comes to my side.

"Miss Chance would like a word."

I hesitate for a moment before looking at Colson. He shrugs in response. We stand up at the same time when the man stops us.

"Just you, miss."

I glare. "He's with me."

"Just you, miss," he repeats.

"He's. With. Me." I repeat as well.

The man only blinks before turning to lead us behind the curtains. Behind them is precisely what you would expect a dressing room to look like. A vanity in the corner with makeup strewn across it, a wardrobe on the opposite wall with clothes on hangers, and possibly the softest-looking couch I had ever seen. Lana sits at her vanity in a silk red robe as she touches up her bright red lipstick. Our eyes meet through the mirror.

"That was impressive control you showed out there." Her voice was soft as a feather with a harsh Romanian accent, somehow also hypnotizing. "How long have you had your power, child?"

I look to Colson as if he knows the exact answer before clearing my throat. "Just a few months."

She huffs as she sets her lipstick down. Standing up, her silk robe flows gracefully behind her as she makes her way in front of us.

"Who in your family had the ability?"

My brows push together at the question. I only shake my head.

"This ability is passed down in generations. The only way to have it is to be born with it in your blood. It appears at different times for everyone. Some young, some older. But, it is not random."

I take a deep breath at her words.

"How do I control it?"

She lets out a laugh.

"My dear, you cannot control the fire. You work with the fire."

What does that even mean? How do I not control it when it moves when I ask and obeys me?

"The fire will not do anything it doesn't want to do. You must build its trust and your strength. It takes time and patience. You cannot force too much at once."

"What do you mean?" I ask.

"If you use too much power before your body is ready, it could be deadly. There will be signs that you are getting to your limits. Your nose will bleed, your vision will become blurry, and you will begin to get dizzy. Once you notice even the most simple of changes, stop. It takes time to build up a tolerance and the trust of the fire."

Lana glides over to sit on her couch, grabbing a glass of champagne from her guard.

"How many of us are there?" Her eyes meet mine as she sips. "I mean, people who have this ability."

"You are the first one I have met in many years. I performed with a man named Victor back in my circus days. An amazing fire dancer he was. But that was when I was very young."

"What happened to him?" Colson's words startled me.

"He pushed his body too far." Sadness flickers in her arctic eyes. "He pushed the flames where they did not wish to go. His body simply could not keep up. It failed." She swirls the liquid around the glass as the memories flood back to her.

"I'm sorry." The words come out with a breath.

Her head snaps back up to me. "It was a long time ago. I vowed that if I ever met someone with the same abilities, I would share my knowledge with them so that it wouldn't happen again. In Victor's memory."

I can see why Colson brought me here. I figured that as soon as she started dancing, but now I really understand. He thought there was a chance that this wasn't all fake and that there could be someone else like me—someone who could help teach me because he couldn't. Then maybe, just maybe, I could control this flame inside of me.

CHAPTER

16

Cas and I stand, heads tilted, as we watch a man stuck at the top of a billboard as two cops yell at him from the ground. Somehow, he had sprayed a massive mural before someone finally noticed and called him in. I couldn't even make out what the mural was. It just has so much going on.

The man protests to the cops, refusing to come down. As we sit and watch, Cap, Austin, and Leo finally appear in the engine. Austin makes his way to us, coming to stand beside me.

"What the fuck is going on?" He asks.

"I'm not sure. But it gets more chaotic the longer you watch."

All three of our heads are tilted to the side, and we are now watching the man and cops scream at each other. The man has removed his shirt and is threatening to take his pants off next. Why? I'm not sure, but it is amusing.

"How did you guys get here in the medic before us?" Austin turns to ask.

"Codi was driving." Cas's monotone voice chimes in.

I tilt my head to look up at Austin, giving him a devious smile.

"Ah, that makes sense."

Someday, I'm going to get in trouble for speeding in the ambulance, but I will forever argue that I am always first to the scene every time.

"Think we're going to be needed?" Austin asks, staring at the man who is now removing his pants.

I sniff. "Probably not. If anything, they'll want us to take him to the hospital to check his mental state."

Both guys let out a chuckle.

We watch a few officers climb the ladder to the billboard's top. Eventually, the officers can apprehend the crazy man, and we can perform a rope rescue, lowering the screaming man down to the ground.

Austin helps me pack up the ropes again as the officers drive the man away.

"So." He breaks the silence.

I glance up at him, raising a brow.

"How was your date with Delose?"

I squint at him. "What do you mean?"

"I saw you guys together the other night."

I continue to squint at him. Was he at the show that night and saw what I did during the performance? Was he at the gym and watched me kick Colsons ass multiple times. God, I hope that's it. That way, he can tease Colson about getting beat up by a girl.

"You guys were driving somewhere. I saw you in his truck."

"Oh!" I try to say like I completely forgot I was even with him. "Yeah, he needed a sparing partner, so we went to the gym."

"At 11 pm?"

Shit...

That was about the time we were coming back from the show. I talked Colson's ear off that long drive back about how incredible that show was and what Lana could do with the flames. It was the most I had ever talked around him. He smiled and listened the whole way, not interrupting or telling me to shut up.

"Uh."

"Hey!" Cap's voice from the front of the engine cuts me off. Or should I say, it saved me from having to explain anything further. "Hurry it up, you two! Lunch is waiting!"

One thing I learned since starting this career is never, and I mean NEVER, keep a firefighter away from a good meal. We hurry up the pace and get back to the station.

After lunch, we cleaned up around the station and then took some time to relax in the recliners, preparing for a possibly busy night. I sit, legs crossed to my side, reading my fantasy smut while the guys argue about what to watch. It's not too often I watch anything with them. Most of the time, they put on horrible comedies or old-time war movies. Sometimes, if I'm too tired to read, I'll stare at the TV, not even paying attention to what's playing, just daydreaming. Just as the guys agree on a movie, the tones go off.

"Station 31, respond to a smoke complaint at 376 Oak St. Caller states there is smoke coming from the old shopping center."

We all get up with a grunt. Most of the time, the smoke complaint calls are nothing. Maybe someone is burning trash in their backyard, and sometimes just steam from a building that people mistake for smoke. Still, it's better than getting our daily call to the nursing home because someone took a tumble out of bed. We throw on our turnouts and head out.

We don't see any smoke as we pull up to the old shopping center, but it's our job to check anyway.

"Codi, Cas, head inside and check the delta side. Austin, Leo, check the alpha side. Report back if you find anything. I'm going to do a 360 of the outside. Should be a quick look over."

"Yes, Cap!" We all shout together.

We head inside with our air tanks strapped to our backs just in case and tools in hand.

The sun has fallen behind the hills behind the old building, causing it to be dark inside the rotting walls. Our flashlights reflect off the puddles from the leaking roof. I can hear our boots crunching as we walk and water dripping in the distance. The smell of rust and mildew is more pungent than any smell I've ever experienced. We split off into our pairs and headed to the side of the building cap assigned us.

"Hey, Code!" Leos's voice comes from behind me as the handle of his axe taps my helmet, rattling my head and causing it to tip to the side slightly since I didn't connect the straps.

"Hey!" I yell, protesting, and adjust my helmet. Even when the helmets are adjustable, my head is so tiny that getting them to fit right is hard.

"No falling through floors, alright? Stay upright."

I roll my eyes and turn back to where we were heading.

Cas and I walk alongside each other, our flashlights occasionally crossing paths. The building is falling apart, and it is almost dangerous for anyone to be inside. They didn't specify what part of the building the so-called smoke was coming from. Occasionally, there would be an old, broken chair along the wall and a pile of lumber, but nothing on fire yet. When Cap said this should be a quick look, I don't think he truly realized how big of a place this is. Without even thinking, I grab the back of Cas's turnouts, yanking him back as his foot starts to break through a wood board, obviously covering a hole in the floor. The board snaps with his weight and falls through the hole as he stumbles back.

"Thanks." He whispers to me as we watch the wood fall into the darkness.

"Uh-huh." I nod, patting his back as we continue.

Several minutes go by, and we find nothing. In the corner of my eye, I thought I saw movement. I stop and shine my light in that direction. I stare for a moment, waiting for something to move. I look back to see Cas hasn't even noticed I stopped and has made his way into the next room, out of my sight. I scoff through my nose and take a step when I hear a noise from where I was looking. I stop again. I scan the area and notice fresh footprints like someone had walked through a puddle. I decide to do the dumbest thing and investigate.

I follow the footprints around a corner to see a shadow avoid my light. I freeze momentarily, then pick up my pace to see someone run through my light.

"Hey!" I scream at them, picking up to a run.

The air tanks and turnouts are definitely meant for something other than running in. In a panic, I strip the air tank off my back and the helmet off my head to reduce weight—my boots thunder on the floor, echoing off the walls. I round the corner, following the figure into a large, empty room. The only thing here are some ropes and cables lying around the floor. I slow my pace down again, shining my light on every inch of this dark room. Nothing.

Where the hell did they go?

I make my way to the middle of the room when I hear cracking under my feet. Before I could even think, "Oh fuck." The floor gives way. I try to find a way to save myself, but instead, my head slams into a piece of concrete that was once part of the floor.

Then, my vision goes dark.

CHAPTER

17

My vision starts fading in and out, and everything becomes blurry when I can see anything again. Everything looks the same when it's blurry. I can't make out which way Is up, but with the feeling of warm blood running down my face, I think I'm upside down. I blink a few times, trying to look up. My leg was wrapped in the ropes that were all over the floor. Somehow, they are caught on something I can't see, holding me in place. My head falls back down, and the blood pounds in my ears. I move slightly, and shooting pain travels up my left leg, which is wrapped in the rope. The only sound I can muster up is an uncomfortable grunt. From the feeling, I would guess my hip is dislocated, and with the sharp pain, I know my knee is definitely fucked up.

"Fuck." I grunt.

I look to the floor and see blood pooling up under me. I bring my hand to my head to feel a sting. I bring my hand back and see blood covering it. I tried to reach for my radio but could not find it in its typical spot. It must have hit the floor when I fell and broke it off my jacket. I try to shout, but it comes out hushed. Any movement sends so much pain shooting through my body. I can hear Leo now.

What did I tell you? No falling through floors again!

Luckily, my light is still pinned on my jacket, swaying along with me. My head is starting to pound with the amount of blood rushing to it. I use all my core strength to try and reach up to undo my leg, but the movement is too painful on my hip. I wince at the pain. My free leg hangs uncomfortably, and my arms dangle by each ear. I'm in such a vulnerable situation. As I begin to accept my fate, I see movement ahead. I squint my eyes as if that will help me see any better. Someone is in the shadows.

"Leo?" My hoarse voice echoes through the darkness.

The figure says nothing but moves closer.

"Say something," I demand.

Still, nothing.

The figure makes its way to my light. A tall, slender man in all black, broad shoulders moves with every step. His hood is up, covering the color of his hair, if he has any. A mask over the lower half of his face, just under his eyes. As he takes another step closer to me, the click of a knife draws my attention.

Shit. Shit. Shit.

This is the guy who attacked me. This has to be the man murdering all these girls. It would make sense being in an abandoned building. Did he dump a body? Was he scoping the place out? Was he the one who called, thinking I would respond to the call? I squirm, but nothing helps. It only causes more pain to shoot through my body, my head pounding harder now.

"Leo!" I try and scream. It's a little louder than my other attempts. "Leo! Help!" I scream again.

There is no sound from above. Has he still not noticed I'm no longer following him? Panic erupts through my body, and my heart races as the masked man gets closer and closer. He lifts his knife as he gets right in front of me. I squeeze my eyes shut and turn my head, hoping this will be over quickly. I'm already in so much pain I don't think anything could make it worse at this point. I feel a slight tug at my ankle, the sound of steel slicing through rope, and then a sharp pain in my left shoulder as I hit the ground hard. A loud grunt leaves my lungs as the air is forced out on impact. My hip slams into the hard ground, and

I wince again. I open my eyes to see I'm lying in my own blood. Black boots block my light as the masked man kneels before me, examining every inch. I try to memorize his face, at least as much as I can see. Thick dark eyebrows, light blue eyes, nearly as bright as mine even in the dark. They gracefully lock on mine, and we gaze at each other for a moment. His gloved hand grazes down my blood-covered cheek as our eyes stay locked.

"Who are you?" I whisper like he's going to give me his full birth name and social security number right here. His head tilts to the side like a dog at the question. He brings one finger to where his mouth would be as if to Shush me. There's something so eerie yet comforting about him. I can see why so many women have become his victims. Something draws me to him even when I know what he is capable of. As if I can tell myself, "he would never do that to me. I'm different. I can change him." I know that's a lie, but my gut still tries to convince me it's true.

I can hear faint radio sounds from above us, but my eyes don't leave the man in fear that he'll be gone when I look back at him. Long, dark eyelashes line his eyes, making it almost look like he's wearing makeup. He runs his hand down my face again, wiping away the blood, points up to where the radio sounds are coming from, and then disappears into the shadows again.

"Dovetch!" Leo's voice echoes down to me, and multiple lights illuminate the area.

The man is nowhere to be found, like a ghost. I try to look up to the guys, but the lights blind me and give me even more of a headache.

"What happened?" Austin shouts.

"I saw someone." My voice was finally clear. "I chased them here and…" I pause, gazing back to where the man once kneeled before me. "I hurt my leg pretty bad. I don't think I can walk on it."

I hear Leo on his radio but can't understand what he's saying. I assume he's calling Cap in for help.

"We're going to get you out of there, alright? Hang tight!" Cas shouts.

"Just stay there," Austin shouts after Leo.

"Thanks. Don't think I have much of a choice now."

I hear Cas chuckle towards Austin. With a leg this badly hurt, talking alone hurts.

Hours later, my hip was back in place after a few nurses and doctors had to hold me down. Cap ran back to the station to get my sweatpants so I could leave the hospital, not in a gown with my ass cheeks for the whole world to see. The nurses managed to help me put them on before putting a huge metal brace around my knee.

"You'll have to wear this for the next six weeks. You can take it off to shower, but that's it. I want to see you back here once a week to make sure everything is healing fine." The doctor had explained to me before getting me discharged. I get to go home with a pair of crutches and practically a robotic leg, but luckily, nothing was severely injured. I'll be out of work for a few weeks, but that won't stop me from going to the station. A young nurse helps me out of bed and into a wheelchair as the sound of frantic running comes from the hallway. I look at the doorway just as Colson slides to a stop.

"What the fuck happened?" He shouts.

The nurse gives him a dirty look at the profanity before leaving the room.

"I got hurt," I say softly, adjusting myself in the wheelchair.

"I can see that. How?"

I take a deep breath and look at Cap, who is still in the room. "Can we have a minute?" I say as sweetly as possible.

He nods and leaves the room, patting Colson's shoulder on the way out.

"He was there," I whisper.

"Kelso?" Colson asks, confused.

"No, Colson!" I shout. "The killer. The killer was there. I chased him through the building when I fell. I was hanging by a rope, and he approached me."

Colson's eyes get so big that I swear life flight could land on them. "Could you see who it was?" He asks.

I shake my head. "He had a mask on."

Colson growls at the answer.

"He didn't hurt me," I say softly.

His head tilts to the side, confused.

"He helped me down. I thought he was going to kill me, but he didn't. He got me down and then stayed with me until help came. He had every opportunity to hurt me or take me, but he didn't."

"So, he didn't touch you?" The dominance in his voice rattles me.

I hesitate for a moment, remembering the feeling of his gloved hand on my face.

"He touched my face."

Anger floods Colson's eyes as he looks down at me.

"That's it. Like, he caressed my face."

"Why?"

"I wish I knew," I answer softly. "Maybe I'm just not his type."

Colson rolls his eyes and walks behind me, grabbing each wheelchair handle.

"Whatever. Let's get you home."

Colson holds the door to my apartment open as I gain balance on the new set of crutches. Cap had been nice enough to grab all my stuff while he headed back to the station to get me a change of clothes so I could go straight home after the hospital. I manage my way to the couch as Colson arranges my stuff.

"You can always come stay with me, you know."

I turn to face him, now standing in my kitchen.

"That way, I can help you."

"Colson." I scoff. "Your house has stairs that will be tough for me to get up and down for a while, and I'm not sleeping on the couch. At least my place is on a single level, and there's an elevator to get up here. I appreciate the offer, though."

It wasn't a lie. I did appreciate it. Colson looks around the apartment, almost defeated, before going to the couch. He sits beside me, lifts my braced leg, and gently lays it across his lap. I grunt, expecting pain, but it's nothing I can't handle.

"I need a shower," I say under my breath.

Colson looks at me and nods.

"I'll leave you to it, then." He says softly.

"Actually." I stop him from getting up.

His brows raise.

"Maybe you can order some food? Then pick a movie, and we can watch it when I get out."

His dark eyes meet mine and lock for a moment.

"I wouldn't mind some company after today."

Something in me didn't want to be alone tonight. Even if the killer didn't hurt me, it still scared me enough to want someone here with me for a while. I'm scared that if I'm left alone, my mind will start going through all the things that could have gone wrong.

In the bathroom, I sit on the toilet, struggling with the new brace wrapping around my bruised and swollen knee. Frustration builds the longer it takes before I finally let some out with a grunt. There's a knock at the bathroom door.

"Yeah?" I yell out.

The door handle clicks open, and Colson peaks his head in.

"Everything ok?"

I clear my throat, look at him, and gesture to the brace entrapping my leg. He chuckles and then walks into the bathroom.

"May I?"

I nod.

He drops to one knee and begins undoing the buckles. I watch the focus on his face, his dark hair hanging over his brow, swaying with every movement. His dark eyes locked on what he was doing. His fingers occasionally grazed my leg through the CWFD sweatpants I wore at the hospital. The last buckle clicked open, and his eyes met mine. The butterflies in my gut started dancing again as our eyes stayed locked.

"Do you need any more help?" His voice was a near whisper.

I take a deep breath, looking over to the faucet.

"Could you turn on the shower for me?"

A smirk grows on his face, and he obeys, standing up to lean over me and turn the water on. Steam fills the room shortly after. He kneels back down in front of me.

"Anything else?"

Take my clothes off and fuck me in this shower.

The voice in my head demands as she sits on her thrown, legs spread and fingers slowly making her way up her thigh.

"I got it from here," I whisper over the sound of the running water.

He simply mouths, "Okay," and leaves the room, shutting the door behind him. He goes back and forth from I need to be the one to take care of you to you are strong and independent. So much that I can't tell how he will react to things anymore. But knowing he is only a call away is comforting.

I begin striping my clothes off, exposing the bruises and dried blood. The gash on my head didn't require stitches, just a few bandages to hold it together. But the surrounding area is black and blue with dried blood through my hair. Random bruises are scattered around my body. I didn't realize how much body fat I had lost this year. My abs are every gym girl's dream, flexing with every labored breath, my shoulders round and rippling with every movement, my arms toned and bulging. No wonder my uniform has been a little more snug lately. Most of the shifts where nothing happened, I spent in the weight room during the day unless Cap gave us some random tasks around the station, so it makes sense that my muscles have gotten bigger. If I'm not lifting weights, I'm running miles.

I pull down the sweatpants to see the damage to my leg. My knee is swollen and blue. I can't even bend it. Bruising ran up my leg from where the rope held on tightly and on my hip, where I landed after being cut down. I never told anyone the feeling I got around the killer. The calmness I felt looking into his eyes like I would have almost trusted him for a moment. I almost feel guilty knowing I felt that way. I knew what this evil bastard could do, yet I gazed into his eyes like he would never hurt a fly. I knew better than that. I keep running through every reason why he wouldn't have killed me. I was hanging there, vulnerable. He could have easily slit my throat, and I would have been gone, unable to do a damn thing. But he cut me down. And even then, I couldn't run. I could barely speak. And he did nothing. Why?

I stare into my blue-grey eyes in the mirror. I don't think I am ugly by any means, but I'm also not beautiful either. I'm just me. I have my father's eyes, hair, nose, and facial structure, but my mother's body type, just far more muscular than hers. I have my mother's stubbornness and my father's determination. And his temper, too. I run my hand over the tattoo lining my collarbone. My father's birthday with his initials. The first tattoo I got when I turned 18. I miss him more than anything.

As the mirror begins to fog up, I limp to the shower, trying my best not to fall and having to call Colson in to help me.

CHAPTER

18

Standing in the dark, old building, the rain outside pounds against what is left of the old windows. Thunder claps, and the wind roars. It's the most significant storm I've seen in years. The smell of smoke overwhelms my senses as the fire slowly grows around me. I wave my hand through the air, the flames following my every move. The sound of broken glass crunching under heavy footsteps comes from behind me. I slowly turn to find a man standing in all black, covered from head to toe, only his bright blue eyes staring down at me. He's so much taller than me.

I blink, and he's closer. Now, mere inches from me. My heart races, but I stand my ground and look deep into his eyes. His hand grazed my face, and I leaned into his touch. His hand cups my jaw, tilting my head to look back at him. His other hand grips my waist, gently pulling me into him. I can feel him. Every inch of him. Hard and against my body. My gut twists as I push into him more—my pulse building between my thighs. I push my breasts against him as his hand travels down my neck to trace just above my right breast. A tingle travels down my spine. He leans closer, and I part my lips to wait for him. A sharp pain erupts in my throat, and I gasp for air, only to be welcomed with a warm liquid. Blood.

Blood fills my mouth, and it pours down my throat, suffocating me. The man takes a step back, and I throw my hand up to find a large knife shoved deep in the center of my throat. I thrash and gasp, getting *no air. I drop to my knees at the feet of this mysterious man. His hand grips the hair on the back of my head, pulling me to look up to him.*

"Good Girl." He growls.

His voice is more profound than anything I've heard, echoing against the walls. My heart races faster as I fight for air while he holds my head to look into his eyes. My mouth drops open with the position I'm put in.

His other hand travels down to his belt, undoing the latch and then the button of his black jeans. I can see him fighting against the fabric, pushing the limits of the stitching. He runs his hand over himself, the fabric getting tighter.

Blood runs down my chin, and he gently rubs his thumb across the trail.

"Open wide, baby girl." He snarls, sliding his free hand into his jeans and gripping himself. He exposes himself, pulling out from behind the denim. He springs free, hard, and already dripping. He grips the hair at the nape of my neck, arching my head back further, causing my mouth to open wider. He forces my lips around him and shoves himself deep into my mouth, nearly hitting the back of my throat. I gag on the blood and throbbing shaft, forcing its way further down my throat. I can't breathe. Panic is erupting inside me, and he pulls in and out. His head is thrown back as a moan escapes. I continue to gag and choke on the blood bubbling up my throat. Blood pours out of my mouth around him, traveling down my chin. He moans louder, grunting with every thrust. He moves faster and faster until he thrusts hard, groaning loudly as he climaxes down my throat. I choke more—too much fluid in my airway.

He pulls out, blood and cum and saliva pour out of me. I gasp again, not getting any air.

"Good girl," he growls again.

He removes the knife still plunged in my throat, then slams it into my chest, through my heart.

I jolt awake, covered in sweat and panting. I frantically claw at my throat to find it in one piece. I gasp for air, only for my lungs to be filled. I'm in my bed with a pillow, elevating my injured leg. The door to my bedroom swings open, and Colson comes rushing in. He franticly scans the room with his gun raised before rushing to my side.

"I'm fine," I say hoarsely.

He drops his gun onto the nightstand and then throws himself down next to me, grabbing onto my shoulders.

"What happened?" He says in a panic.

"Bad dream." I cough, still panicked.

My heart rate begins to slow as Colson holds me closer, rubbing his hand up and down my arm. I start to slow my breathing down as I breathe him in.

Deep breath in, deep breath out.

"Do you want to talk about it?"

I shake my head, not wanting even to remember that dream. It felt so real, which made it that much more fucked up. I don't want to remember that feeling, that panic.

I rest my head against his chest, listening to his racing heartbeat. I throw my hand across his chest, gripping his shoulder.

"Don't leave," I beg. "Stay."

His grip gets tighter as he lays back in the bed, holding me the whole way down. I grip his shirt tightly, holding on for dear life as our heart beats both slow. My head rests on his muscular chest, going up and down with each breath he takes. The feeling of comfort and safety chases away the panic. I flinch as his hand runs through my hair.

As Colson pets my head, my heart finally slows to a resting pace, and sleep overcomes me again.

I sleepily open my eyes as the morning sun shines from my bedroom window. I begin to stretch, but every inch of my body protests at the movement. I wince at the pain.

It takes me more time than usual to get out of bed with the amount of pain flowing through my body. But I managed to follow the smell of freshly brewed coffee into the kitchen.

Colson stands at the stove, coffee in hand, flipping over a pancake. He's still in his jeans from last night. His t-shirt fits snuggly to his chest, the tattoos traveling down his arm exposed. A small dragon tattoo flows behind his ear and then down his neck. His dark hair is still messy from sleep.

My crutches click as I enter the room. I grunt as I gain my balance.

Colson turns to me with a slice of bacon in his mouth, giving me a sleepy smile.

"Coffee?" He murmurs.

I nod my head and head for a chair. After a night full of nightmares and pain, I'm going to need something to keep me somewhat alive. The doctor gave me pain meds, but those things just put me to sleep. I can't sleep the whole day away when I need answers.

A cup of coffee with creamer slides across the counter to stop before me, followed by a plate of pancakes with two slices of bacon. I smother the pancakes in butter and syrup before cutting into them.

"Thank you."

Colson smiles and nods.

"I mean it. Thank you for staying with me last night and taking care of me. You really didn't have to."

"I wanted to." He says softly. His words sincere and caring.

He fixes himself a plate and sits next to me. I clear my throat before taking a bite. Sweet and warm.

"I'd ask how you slept last night, but."

I shrug. He already knows. I probably kept him up all night with the nightmares. Why my brain even came up with any of those is disturbing enough. It was so vivid. I could feel everything. I bring my hand to my throat to only feel smooth skin. No cut or knife. No mixture of body fluids running down. I need to stop reading dark romance books that take things to another extreme. Colson must have carried me to bed last night because I last remember eating Chinese and watching some rom-com with him before the pain meds kicked in, and I drifted off to sleep. He even propped my leg up for me. I'm surprised he stayed after putting me to bed, but I'm glad he did. Having him there after waking up in a panic helped. I wouldn't have been able to get back to sleep without him there. I felt safe. Like nothing in this world could hurt me with him there. But I remembered he doesn't live here. He will have to go home soon or to work, and I'll be left alone again.

"Were you wanting to go home today?" I quietly ask, grabbing my coffee.

He raises a brow at me before responding. "Do you want me to?"

I go back to my food, pushing it around with my fork. How do I tell him I don't want him to leave my side now? I've been so independent, and now I don't want to be left alone.

"Like I said last night, you can stay with me at my place if that would make you feel safer."

It would and wouldn't. It will be a while before I can make it upstairs. But having him there and knowing no one would know where I was would make me feel safe.

"The stairs," I whisper. "And you need to go to work."

He takes a sip before responding.

"I will carry you up those damn stairs. And as for the work situation. I can take you to the station with me, and when I can't, I'll drop you off at the firehouse. That way, you'll never be alone and always have someone there for you."

Shit. He thought this through.

He probably had plenty of time last night while I kept him awake.

"Okay," I whisper.

He looks at me, confused for a moment. I just gave up all my independence so quickly. I fought him every second the first time I went to his house. Now, I'm going willingly.

He lightly sets his coffee down and looks at me.

"Is there anything you'll need to get to be more comfortable?"

I think for a moment. I would need clothes and my bathroom stuff.

"Can we go to a bookstore?" The question comes out almost pitiful. The only thing that could make time go by faster is reading some good books.

He huffs a breath out of his nose and nods.

"Of course we can. When we're done with breakfast, we can go."

I can't help but let a smile grow on my face like a child was told they could have any toy in the store. I don't know why it made me so happy. I could go any time, but having him take me for some reason makes everything more exciting.

CHAPTER

19

Soft music plays over the speakers of the enormous bookstore. The smell of fresh coffee and pastries comes from the back of the store at the small coffee shop. Only a few people are walking around, reading the first few pages of a book to see if they are interested. I immediately limp my way over to the fiction-romance section. Colson follows close behind. I search the shelves, picking multiple books to read over the next few weeks. Walking with crutches and an armful of books is almost more challenging than my CPAT test. I turn around to see Colson is no longer by my side.

Damn it.

I was going to ask him to get me a basket. Several minutes pass, and I try to shuffle to the next section when all the books in my arms fall.

I rest on my crutches, full of frustration. I hold back tears as I look at the pile of books in front of me, and I can't even bend down to pick up when there's a tap on my arm. I look up, expecting a stranger or a worker to ask if I need help. Instead, Colson stands holding a small tablet, gesturing for me to take it. I take it from him, and he bends down to pick up all my dropped books.

"What's this?" I ask, examining the small, matte tablet now in my hand.

"Yours." He says, not taking his eyes off the books he's picking up.

My brows push together in confusion.

"It's an E-reader. You can have all your books in one place and even get new ones instantly. You won't have to wait to go to a store. I know how much you like to stay home, and with your hurt leg, you won't have to get off the couch to get a new book."

"Oh." I continue looking at the small device.

"Here, " he says, reaching out to take it back. He then lays the pile of books out in front of him and starts typing on the tablet.

I look at the covers on the sleeves as Colson does his thing. After what feels like forever, he finally speaks.

"There." He says, handing the E-reader back to me.

I look at him, confused, before he explains.

"All of these books are now downloaded onto this. Let me know if you find any more, and I'll download them, too."

"Don't we have to pay for this thing?" I ask, holding the E-reader out.

"Already paid for." He says softly, placing the pile of books back on the shelves.

"And the books on it?"

"Paid for." He says, turning back to me.

I look down at the slim, matte E-reader in my hands. It holds every book I want to read. I tap on the screen to see words pop up, looking just like a regular page in a book.

"Come on," Colson says, placing his hand on my lower back and pushing me to the coffee shop in the back.

We sit at a table for two, hot coffees in front of us, empty plates that come warm, that fresh baked cookies once sat on. I sit, hypnotized, reading on my new E-reader. Colson sits across from me on his phone, brows furrowed at the screen. I finally looked up and saw that we had been sitting here for almost two hours. I clear my throat, and Colson glances up at me. He has been sitting here for hours while I read, not complaining once. He just allowed me to get lost in my little fantasy world. I smile at him, and he mirrors me.

"Good book?" He asks, nodding his head at the tablet in my hand.

I smile and nod at him, probably the most content I've been in a while, completely forgetting about my pain.

"Would you mind if we moved this to the station? The chief just messaged me, and I need to review some stuff on the case."

"Of course." I nod, shutting off the screen and picking up my coffee.

"I got it." Colson swipes my hand away, picking up my things for me and helping me down the three steps that separate the bookstore and the coffee shop.

Walking into the CWPD station feels like cheating on the fire department. The sound of phones ringing, fingers clicking on keyboards, printers jamming in the corner. It definitely has a different vibe than the firehouse. Colson leans me to his office, a glass window separating his office from the rest of the department, a large wooden desk in the center of the room in front of the large window, and a stove love seat against the wall.

"Make yourself at home. This shouldn't take long."

"No problem," I say, plopping down on the loveseat, turning on my E-reader again, and continuing my book.

Colson sits at his desk, the key clicking under his fingers. After some time, I get tired from reading when I look up at Colson. He has a shocked look on his face, staring at his computer screen.

"Everything okay?" I ask, concerned.

"I might have found him." He whispers.

I sit up straight, waiting for him to explain more.

"There was a body found a while ago, and the security cameras were still active. Even the owners forgot they were still paying for them."

I jump up, limping to Colson's side to watch the videos with him.

"Careful." He says, putting all his attention on me, not using my crutches.

"Show me," I demand as I throw my hand on his shoulder to take some weight off my injured leg.

A few clicks later, the surveillance video pops up on the screen. We both stare intensely, hoping the killer forgot to cover his face this one time. A black sedan pulls up to the back of the old building. Unfortunately for us, the man gets out in his usual attire—black on black with a mask covering his face.

"Damn it." I hiss at the screen.

"Just wait. Do you see that?" Colson says, pointing at the sedan's license plate. "I might be able to track that plate. Hopefully, this guy is dumb enough to use his personal vehicle."

Colson Zooms in on the plate, trying his best to make out the numbers of the pixelated screen.

"I can't..."

"387 HGK. Oregon plates. Tags are going to expire two months from now." I interrupt.

Colson looks at me, shocked. "Alright." He huffs, clicking a few more times.

He pulls up a screen that I am probably not supposed to be looking at. People walk past his office, occasionally glancing at the disabled girl hovering over the detective's shoulder.

"387?"

"387 HGK," I repeat.

He nods, typing the numbers into a tracking system. The screen takes its sweet time loading, searching through all the data, searching for this license plate.

Oh please, give us something. Stolen car, warrant, something we can use to find this monster.

I pray to no one in particular. The screen finally loads, bringing up information I don't understand.

"Car isn't reported stolen." Colson reads. "No warrants, no tickets. Clean record."

"But who does it belong to."

"Lloyd." He reads off.

My heart drops to my stomach as he pulls up the ID photo of the car's owner. Blue eyes staring back at me, Dark hair hanging over his brow, and an innocent-looking smile.

My eyes widen, and I am at a loss for words. My gut twisted, threatening to evacuate my breakfast.

I feel sick.

"No," I whisper, shaking my head. I lose my balance and slam my back against the wall, my good knee buckling.

I want to puke, cry, and rage all at the same time.

It can't be. It can't. There's no way.

I begin to shake uncontrollably.

"What's wrong? Do you know him?"

The name on the ID mocks me, bringing back a flood of emotions. Fear and panic build inside me as I read the name and study the photo of the man I know—the man I used to know better than anyone, who once had my heart.

"That's my ex."

CHAPTER

20

Trevor Matthew Lloyd

The name of my ex is burnt in my mind. There's no way. He may have been manipulative but never aggressive. He never raised even a finger at me. It took a lot for him to even raise his voice at me. This has to be a mistake. Maybe his car was stolen, and he hasn't reported it yet? Flashes from last night erupt in my mind.

His blue eyes stared at me from under the black hood, his hand gracing my blood-covered face, the comfort I felt around him. When thinking back to the masked man kneeling before me, the image of him without the mask flashes.

It's him.

The eyes, the dark brows, the soft gaze at me. There's no denying it. I can sit here and argue all day that he would never do such a thing. But everything is pointing to him. *His* car was registered under his name, his eyes were staring back at me, and his touch was on my face. Even now, looking at the masked man getting out of the car on the surveillance video, it's him. Tall, lean. The walk is the same as his. It makes sense why he didn't hurt me. He still loves me. He said it himself. "You dated this guy?" Colson's voice brings me back to reality.

"Remember when you picked me up from the coffee shop? The guy I was talking to? That's him."

Colson's eyes get huge at the statement. He franticly jumps out of his chair, opening drawers and scraping his badge and gun onto his hip.

"Where are you going?"

"Do you know where he lives?" He charges me, frantic.

"Not anymore. We lived together when we broke up. He was going to move to Oregon but, I guess, backed out. I didn't even know he was in town till that day."

"Do you have his number?"

I'm starting to feel interrogated.

When I broke up with Trevor, I got a new phone and a new number, selling my old phone. The only numbers I kept were those of my family. I never took the time to memorize anyone's numbers. 911 was the only number I should truly have memorized. I never needed to call my mother for anything, and I saw my brothers every few months.

"Social media? Anything?"

"He deleted everything when we broke up. Like he never existed."

Colson growls, turning away from me to pace the room. If I had known Trevor would turn into this person, I would have kept everything. I never expected him to become such a monster. It now makes me wonder if he did this while we were together or if the breakup triggered something in him. Either way, I can't blame myself, right? Just because I wanted to focus on myself doesn't give him the right to kill people.

My gut continues to twist as I watch the video. He pulls a woman out of the passenger seat, hauling her over his shoulder before checking if anyone is around. The video pauses, and I don't notice Colson standing beside me. He punches a few numbers into the landline phone on his desk, and it starts ringing.

"Yes, sir?" A man's voice on the other end answers.

"Paulson... Put an APB out for a 'Trevor Lloyd.' Age 25, 6'1", dark brown hair, blue eyes, slender build. We think he's our killer."

"On it, sir."

Colson hangs up the phone and looks at me, still in shock.

"Are you okay?" He asks softly.

I said nothing. I was staring at the paused video of someone I once loved, someone I slept and woke up next to every morning for years.

"I think I'm going to be sick." The thought came out like a freight train.

Two hands firmly grip my shoulder, leading me to the office chair. A trash bin is then thrown on my lap.

"You're staying at my house until we find Trevor."

I nod.

"Let's go back and get your stuff."

He pats my shoulder and then helps me stand.

The elevator dings as it reaches my floor, my crutches cracking with my weight. Walking down the hall towards my apartment, I notice something sitting in front of my door. A bouquet of flowers and a small box sit delicately placed. On the box is a note addressed to me.

Codi Dovetch.

Colson and I looked at each other, confused for a moment, before I finally bent down to pick up the note, putting all my weight on my still-good leg. I tore open the envelope, pulling out a crisp, white letter.

Dear Codi,
I heard you were hurt on the job.
I wanted to send you something to make you feel better.
You always loved random flowers and your
favorite cookies from Dana's bakery.

This may not help with physical pain, but I
hope it makes your heart feel good.
Hope to see you around again.
Love and miss you,
-T

My heart drops as I read the letter. Trevor was here, at my home. He doesn't know that I know what he's done. I know it was him who cut me down. That Colson is on the verge of killing him himself now.

Colson rips the letter out of my hands, nearly giving me a paper cut in the process.

"That fucker was here? He knows where you live?" His voice came out as a growl.

I glance around the hallway, hoping he is still around, but no one is there.

"Fuck it." He snarls. "I'm going to send someone to get your things. We're not taking a chance on him being in there waiting for you."

"Do you think he would break into my apartment after leaving stuff outside my door?"

"I'm not taking the chance." He snaps.

"I don't want a stranger going through my things." I protest.

"Then I will buy you all new stuff and have it delivered to my house. You can pick out whatever you want or need. But I'm getting you out of here for now, especially since you can't defend yourself while being injured."

His hand travels to my lower back again, pushing me back to the elevator.

"Wait!" I shout, spinning around out of his grasp.

I hop over and pick up the small box by the flowers.

"I'm not wasting these cookies."

The box is sealed to avoid tampering, so I doubt Trevor did anything to them. And I can't just leave these to get cold.

Colson looked down at the box and then at me. Knowing he would never win the argument that was about to take place, he caved and escorted me out of the building.

"You dated this guy?!" Austin shouts across the fire station's dining table over photos of Trevor's face.

I roll my eyes in response.

"Damn." Cas chimes in. "I always forget serial killers lived normal lives before going fucking savage."

"Okay, guys. We brought you these photos to get a good look at him and to keep an eye out, not judge my taste in men." I shout, slamming one hand on the table.

"I mean, it is pretty shit." Leo's voice echoes out from the kitchen.

I twist my head to glare at him before showing him my favorite finger.

Colson leans quietly against the wall, examining everything on the table before us, tattooed arms crossed over his chest.

"So, basically, we need to babysit Dovetch while you're at work to make sure her psycho ex doesn't come around." Cap's deep voice directed at Colson.

"Hey!" I shout again. "Don't say babysit. I'm not a child."

I decently feel like one. Two parents fighting over what days the other has to watch me.

"Codi, you're injured. You need supervision."

I slap Austin's hand off my shoulder and glare. He wasn't wrong. I am injured and can't do a whole lot by myself. But the doctor said I should be able to walk again once the swelling goes down, which should be in a few days if I do what I am supposed to. At least, I hope.

I try to bend my braced knee only to be met with resistance from the swelling. Leo tosses a bag of frozen corn in my direction, gesturing to my leg extended across a chair. I give him a smirk of gratitude.

The bruising is slowly fading away but remains across my face, arms, and legs.

After some casual conversation and filling me in on the calls I've missed, the sun has set, and the frozen corn has thawed on my leg.

"As fun as this is, I need to get Miss Peg Leg here home to rest."

I glare at Colson for the nickname. But I won't argue since I've been sitting in this wooden chair for hours now, and my ass is going numb. All I want now is to take my pain meds, read, and eventually pass out.

CHAPTER

21

I hobble down the stairs, following the sound of Colson flipping papers at the dining table next to the kitchen. After a few days of heavy rest, I can put a little weight on my left leg now, but not without a severe limp. I should still be using the crutches, but they've done nothing but hurt and bruise my armpits. Id rather limp around than deal with that. I shuffle into Colson's sight, and he glares, noticing the missing crutches.

"You're not supposed to be walking on that yet." He grumbles, staring me down through his dark brows.

Staying with Colson has been interesting, to say the least, this week. He sleeps on the floor on a mattress pad while I take up the comfy queen-size bed—way more comfortable than mine. He refused to sleep on the couch downstairs, saying, "I'm too far away in case something happens."

On one hand, it's nice to know someone is there. The nightmares are still frequent. But now I only see Trevor's face instead of a masked figure. I'm not going to lie- I preferred the mask.

I pranced to the kitchen to pour myself a cup of coffee, grabbing the creamer from the fridge.

"Anything new?" I ask, referring to the pile of papers in front of him.

There has been no sign of Trevor since the package was left at my apartment door. Not even another murder.

Colson shakes his head, bringing his cup to his lips. I lean against the kitchen island, giving my leg a break, when my phone buzzes on the counter. I read the messages and immediately regretted reading them.

"Fuck.." I hiss.

Colson glances up at me, brows raised.

"My mom's birthday is this weekend. I completely forgot."

I toss my phone, letting it slide across the counter.

"And.. that's a bad thing?" Colson asks cautiously.

"We normally do a family dinner. It normally ends up in someone leaving early."

It's more like leaving before a full fistfight breaks out. And that someone is me. The last time we had a family dinner was when I finally broke the news that I broke up with Trevor and got accepted into the fire academy. Needless to say, Mom was not thrilled. She loved Trevor like her own and expected us to get married. I guess she'll rethink that once the news comes out that he has been killing people in his spare time.

Colson continues to stare at me.

"I don't even have a car anymore, so I won't be going," I explain.

"I can drive you."

"You don't want to be around my family."

I don't want him around my family. If I brought a guy home to my mother's birthday dinner, they would bombard him with way too personal questions. They would immediately assume we are dating, and when they find out we're not, they would spend the rest of the evening asking why we aren't or trying to convince us to.

"Then you can take my truck." He says, gesturing to the keys on the kitchen island.

I look at him confused, brows pushed together. He shakes his head lightly, waiting for me to explain my confusion.

"You're going to let me go alone?"

He leans back in his chair and takes a deep breath before responding.

"My truck has GPS. Besides, I think your brothers would ensure you are safe while you're there."

He's not wrong. My brothers have always been protective of me.

I take a deep breath, considering his offer. If I don't go, my family will blow up my phone for days, and I will never hear the end of it from my mother.

I am surprised that Colson would allow me to go that far without supervision. If traffic is alright, my parents' house is about a 40-minute drive from Colson's place.

"Are you sure?"

Colson nods, not even looking up at me.

Someone is in a mood this morning.

"Okay," I say, breathy, sipping my coffee.

I still had a few more days before I needed to be there, so that gave my leg more of a chance to heal so I could walk on it better. I won't be able to hide the huge, metal brace from my mid-thigh, over my knee, then halfway down my calf. It stands out a lot against my denim jeans. This is also the first day I've worn jeans instead of sweatpants or leggings. I actually did my hair and make-up today, too, which is a sign that I'm starting to feel better. I'm hoping Colson doesn't smell his hair products on me. They were just on the counter, and I couldn't resist trying them.

I limp over to sit in the chair next to Colson, who is slumped over his paperwork in a pair of light, ripped-up jeans and a black hoodie. He only side-eye glances at me as I plop down in the chair, not being graceful at all, nearly spilling some coffee.

"Careful." He grumbles.

"I'm okay."

I look down at the paperwork laid out on the table.

Reports for every crime scene, including the calls I had been on, crime scene photos, information on Trevor, and more papers I'm sure I'm not supposed to see. I push around some documents as Colson watches me curiously but does not stop me. I uncover a photo that I recognize.

A picture of Trevor and I sits before me, bringing about memories.

"I remember this day," I say softly.

Colson continues to examine me as I lift the photo.

We sit on the beach, his arm around my shoulders, holding me close, a huge smile on both faces. My hair was so long, nearly down to my ass. I sometimes forget how much I chopped off for the academy. In the photo, it blows in the ocean winds. I can almost smell the salty air again. The ring he had custom-made for me on my left-hand rests on Trevor's chest. I stare at the ring in the photo. I glance down at the crime scene photos to see the one of Rachel Linwood's butchered body—the same ring on her hand.

"That was my ring," I whispered, tilting my head to the side.

My gut begins to twist, realizing that Trevor not only killed this poor girl but gave her *my* ring before doing so.

"It was a promise ring he made for me at work," I explain.

I set the photo back down onto the pile of paperwork, slowly grabbing the documents and covering the happy faces. It sickens me to know that someone I had once loved could do such horrible things. We had grown up together, lived, cried, and laughed together. There are so many memories I used to look back on and smile. I now want to vomit thinking about them. The past few days, I've tried to play it off like it didn't bother me, but deep down, it's fucked me up. I used to sleep next to this man every night. I shared an apartment with him until the day we broke up. We had talked about getting married and starting a family together. He held me the night we found out my dad had died. He held me for weeks while I cried and even at the funeral. He was at every Christmas for years. I had let this monster in my home, I'm my life, in my family, in me.

I can feel Colson's gaze as I sit back in my chair.

"Are you sure you don't want me to go with you to your moms?" He asks so gently.

I nod. "I'll be ok."

It's half a lie. I would have to plaster on a smile around my family while I know secrets. But then again, I've done that before. I know my mother is going to bring up the fact that I got hurt and how if I had just stayed with Trevor and not gotten into the fire, this never would have happened, which is likely going to end up in a fight again.

Ever since my dad passed, my mother and I have had a rough relationship, probably because I grew up to be so much like my father. Stubborn, mostly. She loved my father more than anything in the world. Probably more than her children. He was as much her world as he was mine. When he died, something in her died with him. She buried a piece of her. She resented the fact that I wanted to follow in his footsteps. Fire had taken one part of her. She wouldn't survive if it took anything else. My brothers quietly supported me in the background, too scared to do it themselves in fear of disappointing Mom anymore.

I took a deep breath, letting my lungs fill as far as they could before letting it out with a sigh.

"Let's do something today." My voice is a little more cheerful.

I didn't know what it was. It was just something to take my mind off everything and mentally prepare myself for the weekend—an evening with my mother.

CHAPTER

22

It's been a while since I was behind the wheel of something other than an ambulance. Colson's Denali drove smoothly down the highway. The engine is purring under Bad Omens playing over the stereo. I made sure to get a haircut before today. If I didn't, Mom would say some snide comment about it. I turn into a suburban neighborhood. The neighborhood I grew up in. On the streets where my dad taught me to ride a bike, I drew flowers in chalk on the sidewalks, played with the neighbor kids on warm summer days, and chased the ice cream truck. Parking along the sidewalk, I look up to my childhood home. The front yard was professionally mowed, and the flowers were bright, pastel colors—the white siding was clean and free of any spots, with dark-colored shutters framing the windows. The two-story home stood beautiful. The covered porch is freshly painted and clean. I don't see any cars in the driveway. I must be the first one here.

I hop out of the truck and limp up the path to the front door. Fumbling my keys, I find the one meant for my parent's house. I always keep a spare key in case of moments like this.

I am not sure why Mom always does this. She Invites us all over for dinner but gets take-out instead of anyone cooking. Whatever works.

I step into the home, which is decorated the same as the day I moved out. The large living room is to my right, the dining room is to my left, and the stairs are straight ahead.

"Mom?" I call out, just in case.

No response.

I wander around the home, looking at all the old baby photos of my brothers and me. They are all so cute and innocent. I make a loop and return to the stairs, looking up at the hallway leading to the bedrooms and...

My father's study.

I glance around the empty house one more time before attempting the stairs. My knee aches with every step. After gritting my teeth with every movement of my leg, I limp to the closed door at the end of the hall. I graze my fingertips along the white, painted door, then grab onto the handle and twist. The smell of my father's cologne wafts past me as the door swings open. A large wooden desk sits in the center of the room with a computer and papers scattered around it. Cardboard boxes line the walls holding all my dad's things: old clothes, hats, shoes, nic-nacs, and books. Any photo of my dad was stored in this room and locked away. "They're too difficult to look at daily," my mom always said.

I crouch on the floor in front of the box full of my dad's old fire stuff. My knee cracks, and the brace whines as I bend down. I pull a framed photo of my dad leaning against the fire engine. His smile is so big it makes his eyes squint, his muscular arms crossed over his chest. He was such a handsome man. The next framed photo is of him with his crew. I recognize these faces from over the years, but I work with none of them now. Several plaques awarding his accomplishments. Finally, I pull out his name tag.

Dovetch

The same tag I wear on my chest—the name I carry. Another framed photo catches my eye at the bottom of the box. My heart hurts as I stare at the picture of my dad holding me when I was a baby, with a big smile on my face and his—way too big for me—helmet on my head. I bite my bottom lip, holding back the tears.

Two hands firmly grab my shoulder, shaking me slightly.

"Give me all your money!" The voice shouts.

I jump, my breath getting caught in my throat.

"Damn it, Claire," I grunt as the hands turn from a firm grip to a loving hug.

"Hey, sis!" She cheers. "I missed you."

Claire sits cross-legged next to me, her long blonde hair following her down.

"Is that your new truck I saw outside?" She asks.

"Uh." I hesitated for a moment to figure out how to word the response. "No, it's a friend's. He let me borrow it for the day."

"He?" She asks louder than necessary.

Here we go…

"Yes, he. He is my friend."

"Friend? Like.. a boyfriend?"

I roll my eyes. "No. Just a friend."

She holds a stare for longer than comfortable.

"He's been helping me out since I got hurt."

"Is he one of the firefighters?"

"No. Detective."

Her eyes get wide. "A detective?"

I sigh while tilting my head towards her when two hands slam on the door frame.

"Hey, Mom's home. Might want to get out of Dad's office before she sees and freaks out."

Dylan stands tall in the doorway. His green flannel hugged his muscular arms, his dark brown, nearly black hair shone in the hallway lights, and his sharp jaw flexed with every word.

Claire helps me to my feet, and we leave the office, ensuring the door shuts behind us.

My knee aches as I hobble down each step. I get halfway down when the front door swings open. The clacking of heels announces my mother's entrance before she even comes into view. Her dark blue eyes meet mine, and she stops. Her eyes immediately drift down to my brace.

"What happened to you?" The question monotone.

I know if I tell the truth, the arguments will start early, so I avoid the confrontation as best I can.

I lie.

"I was playing basketball with the guys and tweeted my knee. No big deal."

I don't play basketball, but I hope she doesn't realize that.

She huffs a breath and proceeds to take bags of food into the kitchen.

We all sit at the large wooden dining table, Chinese takeout scattered in front of us. We listened to the kids tell us about school and all their new hobbies for an hour. I sit quietly at the opposite end of the table as my mom, in my dad's old seat. Silence falls over the table as the kids finish talking. My mother's eyes shoot at me.

"So, Codi." She says. "How is everything with you?"

I didn't expect her to have any interest in my life.

"Uh…" I hesitate. "Great. The guys I work with are amazing and have become like another family."

"Yes, because you need another family." She grunts.

"Mom." Dylan's voice scolds.

Dylan is the oldest and always the most protective of me, even when It comes to mom.

I took a deep breath and continued.

"The job itself is great. I feel like I help people every day."

"While nearly getting yourself killed." Mom interrupts.

My eyes jet to her. All eyes jet to her. Tyler and Becca, who haven't said much this whole time, glare at my mom. Dylan slams his fork down onto his plate. Jack, Hayden, and Carter all cower their heads down.

"Most parents would be proud of this career."

Her eyes shoot to me, brows pushed together. Her pale blonde hair falls over her shoulder before she responds.

"Not sure how I can be proud of such a foolish choice. You should have just married Trevor and started a family like your brothers."

"Foolish?" I spit. Frustration was boiling inside me. "It's foolish to follow in Dad's footsteps and save lives like him? And guess what, Mom, Trevor is wanted by the police. He's been the one killing all the women in Clearwater. So maybe you should be happy I didn't marry him."

Information I definitely should not have spewed out.

The silence in the room is deafening as everyone's eyes grow wide and shoot at me.

"Well, if you wouldn't have broken his heart, you could selfishly become like your father."

I can feel my face becoming red with anger.

"So you're blaming me for him being a serial killer? Are you kidding me?"

She shrugs.

"Mom, seriously. Just stop." Tyler finally chimes in.

"You won't be thinking that when she gets herself killed like your father. You'll tell me I was right to think it's foolish."

I slam my hands down on the table, nearly knocking over every glass.

"You're not the only one upset that Dad is gone." I snarl at my mother. "Dad was a hero to many people, including his children. I followed in his footsteps because I dreamed of becoming a firefighter. To be a hero like my dad. And I'm sorry, Mom if you hate that, but I love my job, and no matter how many times I get hurt or nearly die on the job, I wouldn't trade it for anything in the world."

And I wouldn't. I love my job, the guys I work with, and the patients we care for. It really is the best job in the world, and if I die doing it, at least I will die doing what I love.

Mom stares at me, her eyes filling with anger.

"You're just like your father. When you die like him, I will not be there to mourn the loss again."

I slam my hands down again, knocking over my glass of wine. I kick the chair out from behind me and storm out of the house, slamming the door loudly.

As I leave the house, I can hear Tyler say. "What the fuck, Mom?"

I limp back to Colson's truck, fumbling the keys to unlock it.

"Code!" Dylan's voice calls out to me.

I whirl around as I reach the truck's tailgate to see my oldest brother jogging towards me.

If I had a few of my father's features, Dylan was a perfect replica of him. Tall, muscular build, sharp jaw line, near black hair. The only thing he got from our mother was her dark blue eyes instead of the Arctic blue my father and I share. I'm the only one of the children who got Arctic blue eyes, along with my oldest nephew, Jack.

"Don't listen to mom." He pants. "She's just.."

"Grieving?" I interrupt.

Dylan cocks his head at me. "You know how she is."

"I liked her better when Dad was alive."

"We all did." He takes a deep breath. "For what it's worth, I'm extremely proud of you. And I know Tyler, Claire, and Becca all are too. Even if they don't say it often."

"Thank you," I say softly.

"And I know Dad would be so proud as well. I wish I had the balls to do it."

I nod.

I know I'm the only one of the kids who didn't listen to Mom and got into the fire service. Dylan even wanted to go into the military at one point, but Mom shut him down. By the time he was old enough to enlist himself, he met Claire. He couldn't bear to leave her for that long.

"I know," I say as a breath. "I'm gonna head home, though."

I turn to the driver's side of the truck when he stops me again.

"Is that true about Trevor?"

I freeze, then nod. "He was caught on surveillance camera of an abandoned building pulling a girl out of his car."

"God…" He breathes, running a hand through his dark hair. "And your leg wasn't from basketball, was it?'

He always had a way of seeing right through my lies, even when I thought the acting was Oscar-worthy.

I shake my head.

"Did he do this?" He growls.

"No! I mean kinda, but no."

His brows push together, confused by my answer.

"I saw him on a call and chased after him, but I fell, got caught on some hanging rope, and got stuck there. I dislocated my hip and fucked up my knee. He cut me down."

He continues to look at me, confused.

"I know, I'm confused too. But I'll text you when I get home. And I'll let you know what else we find out. Okay?"

He nods, reaching out for a hug.

I wrap my arms around his firm body, my face barely reaching his shoulders. He kisses the top of my head.

"Love you, sis." He whispers into my hair.

"Love you too, bro."

I drove home silently, trying my best not to recap the evening. The words my mother had said hit me like daggers. I couldn't believe the things she said to me about my dad.

I return to Colson's house, the headlights illuminating the front porch and garage. I throw the truck in park and shut off the engine, but I don't get out yet. I sit and stare forward for a while, losing track of time, when I see the motion in the corner of my eye.

The front door swings open, and Colson steps out, looking concerned. I take a deep breath before opening the door.

Colson meets me halfway. I think he can tell something is wrong, but he says nothing.

I stopped before him when all my emotions hit me all at once. I burst into tears, falling into his arms. He pulls me closer to him as I let go into his chest. I can't control my breathing as I sob, digging my fingers into his muscular back. His hand holds my head, and he whispers into my hair.

"It's alright. I'm here."

For some reason, his words help relieve the sting of my mothers. I grip him tighter, pushing my wet with tears face into him.

Inside, I sit on the couch, face buried in the palms of my hands, when something taps my shoulder. I look up to see Colson holding a cup of some sort of golden liquid and one round ice cube.

"What's this?" I ask, meeting his eyes.

"Whiskey." He responds, sitting down next to me. "I figured you would need something stronger than tea tonight."

He wasn't wrong, but at the same time, I expected it. Those kinds of fights always happen with my mother around.

I chug down the Whiskey in one shot. It burns on its way down.

"Oh." I cough. "That's got a bite to it."

Colson chuckles and leans back, throwing one foot over his knee.

I hold the glass in my hand and swirl the ice around.

"My mom hates me," I whisper.

"I doubt that."

"She says I'm just like my dad."

Colson takes a breath before responding. "Well, she loved your dad, right?"

I shrug. "She did. Until he died."

Colson says nothing. I don't know what he could say anyway. Without thinking, I pulled out the name tag I had stashed in my pocket without being noticed. I twirl it around in my hand, watching the light dance off it.

"He used to call me his Princess of Fire."

Colson continues to watch me.

"He was my best friend."

CHAPTER

23

Today was the first reasonably sunny day all week. Birds started emerging and dancing from tree to tree, singing the whole way. I spent most of the day sitting on the back patio, which has a beautiful view of the forest behind Colson's house, while he did some work inside.

The sliding glass door slides open, and I turn to look over my shoulder. My sunglasses reflect the late afternoon sun right into Colson's eyes.

He squints with the sodden assault of light.

"I'm heading to the fire station for a little bit. You want to come with?"

I gasp in excitement and jump to my feet faster than I have since my injury. With my leg feeling much better now, I'm willing to test my limits.

Colson chuckles and steps aside, letting me skip past him.

I burst into the fire station doors to find the guys huddled around the kitchen island.

"What's up bitches!" I shout.

They all cheer and run to me, lifting me in a hug.

"Alright, guys." Cap calls out. "Careful with her."

"I'm good, Cap!" I call back. "Shouldn't be much longer in this thing, and I can return to work."

"It's no rush, Dovetch. Make sure you're 100% before you decide to come back. We don't need to rescue you again."

I glare at him but don't argue. He has a point.

If my knee gives out in a fire because I rushed the healing process, I'm not only putting my life in danger but the rest of the crew, too.

Colson's phone rings behind me as the guys fill me in on some exciting calls they've had while I am gone. I almost forgot he followed me in.

"Delose." He says firmly. I only hear him be professional when he's on the phone or barking orders. His voice always seems so soft when speaking to me until I piss him off with my stubbornness.

He returns a few minutes later, putting a hand on my shoulder.

"I have to run to my office for a little while. Are you okay to stay here?"

"Hell yeah!" Austin shouts. "She can help us with dinner!"

I roll my eyes and look back to Colson.

"Yeah, I'm good here. Don't worry about me. Go to work."

He nods, waving to the guys before running out.

Hours go by without a word from Colson, but I'm fine with that now. There haven't been any calls since I was dropped off, so I can catch up on all the stories of the calls I've missed. Joining my crew for dinner and watching Leo's random movies is a nice change. But just as I'm getting comfortable again, the tones go off.

Structor fire at the 1876 Jackson Street. Multiple units requested.

1876 Jackson Street. "That's the police station," I say out loud, jumping to my feet.

The guys rush past me, hurrying for their turnouts.

"Cap!" I call out as he passes me. "Can I come with you? Please? Just as a ride-along?" My voice is practically begging.

He sighs but nods. "You stay out of everyone's way. You are strictly a ride-along tonight."

I nod. I can, if anything, help the rehab unit take care of crews coming out of the fire. Today was a good day to wear my CWFD quarter zip.

I tried calling Colson in the engine, but there was no answer. Dispatch said there were no reports of anyone still in the building, so I'm hoping he just left his phone behind on the way out. We turn onto Jackson Street to be met with a crowd of people and...

Holy shit.

Flames shoot out of multiple windows of the police station. The three-story building is completely engulfed, devouring every bit of empty space. As we slow to a stop, I wait for the guys to rush out and get to work, scanning the crowd for Colson.

He's not here.

Maybe he was out doing something or on his way back to pick me up, and I just missed him. My gut twists as I try to think of any possibility of him not being inside the burning building. I slide out of the engine, my knee stinging a bit at the impact. I continue to scan the crowd with no luck when I see a few people rushing out of the building. I limp as quickly as I can to them.

"Is everyone out?!" I shout.

"I don't know." The hysterical woman responds.

"I'm looking for my friend. Colson." She looks at me, confused. "Detective Colson Delose. Is he still in there?!"

She shrugs her shoulders. "Detectives are on a different floor than me. I wouldn't know."

Some help you are, lady.

I usher her to the EMTs standing by and look back to the building. The firefighters have begun putting water on the flames from the outside, preparing to make entry. I scan the crown one last time, not seeing him, when I look towards the gated parking lot. Both his truck and his work car are parked in their designated spots. Panic starts building up inside me.

Shit. Shit. Shit.

He's inside. I have to tell someone.

I grab a firefighter as he passes by and shout.

"People are still in there!" He only shrugs me off and rushes to aid in putting out the fire.

Asshole.

Obviously, not anyone from my station. I can't even see where the guys went to let them know. Firefighters are rushing everywhere, and all look the same in the heat of the moment.

No pun intended.

Suddenly, the dumbest idea pops into my head. One, I know I will get in a load of trouble for coming up with. But I can't just stand here and hope someone trusts what I say and goes in to check.

I look at the building as the flames lick the red bricks outside. The front door is clear. My eyes drifted to find Cap, and his back finally turned to me, talking to Chief Fitz. They will both have my head for what I'm about to do. I might get fired for this as well. But I can't waste any more time when I have the ability to clear my own path,

I look back to the front door, and suddenly, I'm in a sprint. I hear Cap shout my name as I reach the door, but I'm already in.

The flames eat away at the walls and wooden desks in offices. I throw my hands up and command the fire to clear my path. They obey. I find the stairs, making the flames shift. My knees scream at me as I double-step up to the third floor. When I reach the top, my left knee threatens to give out, screaming in protest. My doctor is not going to be happy to hear this story.

The door to the third floor is shut. I reach for the handle, but my hand sizzles trying to open it. I take a few steps back, breaking out into a full sprint again, slamming my body weight into the weak spot of the door. It swings open, exposing even more flames. The sprinkler system should be on. Why isn't it on?

"Colson!" I shout over the roar of the flames and the alarm system blaring. The smoke attempting to choke me. I cough.

I look to where his office is to see the door open, but no one is inside.

"Colson!" I shout again frantically.

I begin coughing and choking on the smoke as it burns my throat. Controlling the flames only goes so far until the smoke hits you. I scan the floor to find a pair of boots.

I squeal as I run to where they are. Laying next to his desk, Colson lies motionless on the floor. Coughing, I fall to his side.

"Colson, come on!" I choke.

A small grunt comes from him, and I know he's still alive.

I grab his arms and try my best to get him up.

"Colson, get up! We have to go!" I scream.

"Codi?" He coughs.

"Yeah, it's me. You have to get up."

He begins shooing me away. "Codi, get out of here." He demands.

"Get your ass up, now!" I shout. My voice sounded more demanding than I expected. "GET. UP!"

Our eyes meet momentarily, and he reaches his hands and knees.

"There you go."

"Go." He chokes again. "Get out of here."

Frustration erupts in me as I grab his arm and yank him as hard as I can.

"Colson, you get your fucking ass up right now, or we both will die here."

He grunts but starts to make his way to his feet when I hear cracking above us. I look up to see the ceiling giving out under the intense heat. I throw my hands up as drywall and insulation crash toward us rapidly. I force the flames to build a wall above us, halting the mid-air debris—weight ponds down on me like I'm holding everything up with my bare hands. I grunt under the weight, slowly dropping to my one good knee. Colson, still halfway on the floor, looks up to see the dome of flames covering us. I grunt again and push my body further to lift the debris away and throw it across the room.

"GO!" I scream at him.

He grabs my arm as he starts his way to the stairs. My legs are weak, but I keep running. Colson comes to a halt at the stairs when he sees the fire devouring the staircase. I charge past him, throwing my hands up, and the flames clear a path, lining the walls far enough for us to pass. I grab his hand and lead him down to the first floor, keeping a hand up to clear the flames. Alarms blared over the crackling as we burst through the doors.

The cold, outside air slaps us in the face, entering my smoke-filled lungs. I cough as I catch the attention of firefighters.

"Dovetch!" Cap screams out at me, angry but also relieved.

At that moment, I saw the firefighter, to whom I desperately pleaded to go in and save Colson, only to be brushed off.

"You!' I shout, releasing Colson's arm that I didn't even realize I was still holding. "What the fuck is wrong with you!"

The man looks at me, stunned.

"I told you someone was trapped in there! You did nothing! Didn't even tell anyone else."

Without thinking, I rip his helmet from his hand, slamming it to the ground. Anger fills me as the man continues to look at me in shock.

"I'm off the clock, unable to work, but I was still able to go in there and do *your* job!"

"Codi…" I hear Colson's voice say softly.

"You didn't even care that someone was dying in there!"

"Codi…" His voice calls out again.

"You selfish mother fucker."

"Codi!"

"What!" I scream, turning to face Colson.

He gestures to his nose. I stand confused until I feel the warm liquid on my upper lip. I lift my hand and bring it back to my sight to see thick, red blood running down my fingers. My hand is shaking. I figured it was my adrenaline and anger when I noticed my whole body was vibrating more than it usually does after a fire. I can feel the blood rushing from both nostrils, dripping down to my chin. I look up at Colson, eyes wide as both my knees buckle, and I fall to the ground. Multiple hands rush to catch me before I hit the concrete, and everything gets blurry.

CHAPTER

24

"I'm fine!" I shout, pulling my arms away from the paramedics attempting to start an IV in my right arm.

"Codi, your nose was gushing blood, and you nearly passed out."

"It was the adrenaline."

I know it wasn't. I know for a fact that it was from overusing my powers. But what else was I supposed to do? Let the ceiling fall and kill us both? Hell no.

I push off the gurney and try to make my way to the back doors, still wide open, where Colson leans.

"Codi." He coughs.

"Colson." I glare. "I'm good. Seriously, I want to go home."

That was the first time I referred to his house as *home*. I haven't been back to my apartment in a long while. At this point, all I want is to take a shower and go to sleep.

Colson tilts his head at me, hoping it will make me change my mind, but I'm stubborn tonight.

After signing the refusal form for the paramedics, we make it back to the house. The solar lights trailing to the front door glow lightly, reflecting off the damp pathway. Colson unlocks the door and lets me pass through first. He hasn't said a word the whole way back. I stop in the entryway as he locks the door behind him. He empties his pockets on the small table against the wall.

"Colson," I say softly, wanting him to say something. Anything.

He simply responds with a *Hmm?* Not even looking up at me.

"Are you okay?"

He stills for a moment. "Yeah." He whispers.

I'm not sure what else to say. Before I could even think of something, he gripped my shoulders, pulling me into his chest, tightly holding me against him. I freeze momentarily, then wrap my arms around him, gripping his back. He reeks of smoke and sweat, but I ignore it. We both smell like death.

"Thank you." He whispers into the top of my head.

My heart aches at the tone of his voice, still coming down from the fear of almost dying.

I bury my face in him more before responding.

"Of course."

He pushes me slightly away to cup my face in his hands.

"Seriously." He says, looking me deep in my eyes. "I'm beyond furious that you put yourself in that much danger but forever grateful. You saved my life."

I blink multiple times, pushing the tears building up away.

I clear my throat. "You should shower."

My eyes drift to his ash-covered chest.

"So should you." He whispers, his hands still holding each side of my cheeks, I'm sure feeling them heat at his touch.

For a moment, I forgot how to breathe. "You first." I faintly laugh.

His eyes drift, running up and down me. His hands drop from my face before taking a step towards the stairs. I go to the bedroom not long after him and sit on the bed. I look down at my black and white, ash-covered knees.

"Hey, Colson?" I call out to the bathroom.

"Yeah?" He shouts back.

"Before you get in the shower, could you help me take my brace off?"

After the amount of time I've had the brace on, I know how to take it off with no problem. But something in me wants him to touch me again.

He appears in the bathroom doorway with no shirt on, the shadows defining every muscle along his chest and abdomen. My heart races and my face flushes as I look at this man standing before me. He nods, walks over to me, and then kneels, taking my left leg in his hand before unbuckling my brace. His fingers lightly graze my leg as he works, sending a tingling sensation to a very sensitive spot. He pulls the brace off, exposing my leg. His eyes dart up to me, darker than the last time. He runs his hand down my inner thigh, sending shock waves through my body. I wonder if he knows what his touch does to me and if he's doing this purposefully.

"Better?" He purrs.

I nod. "Thank you."

His hand hesitates on my thigh before he finally stands up and starts back to the bathroom, undoing his belt on the way. Simply, the sound of the belt being undone does something to me. The twisting feeling grows in my stomach, going down. My heart races more as I listen to him turn the water on. Moments later, I hear his belt and pants hit the floor, and the curtains slide. My body begins to heat up, so I take my jacket off, my shirt peeling off with it. I stared at it in my lap for a moment, my body temperature only skyrocketing.

Go to him.

The little voice in my head whispers to me. I close my eyes, allowing my inner goddess to take over. Her smile grows wicked, her eyes darkening.

My eyes jet open in a burst of bravery, and I burst to my feet.

Stepping into the bathroom, the fog has already started to fill the room. The smell of his body wash overpowers me. My heart is about to burst out of my chest, but I continue. I can see his silhouette behind the curtain.

I hold my breath as I reach for the curtain, grip it, and quickly slide it open.

Colson turns to me, blinking the water away as it hits his chest, running down his toned body. Our eyes lock, confusion on his face. I take a deep breath and step inside, pushing my body close to his. He doesn't back away, only looks down at me, waiting for my next move. The shower water soaks my legs and bra, warming my body even more. I lift my hands to his chest, running them along the tattoos covering him, brushing away the bit of dirt that is still left behind. He continues to study my face, taking a small step towards me, our bodies pushing together, my breasts being squeezed against him with every breath. I feel his hands make their way to my waist, sending another shock up my spine.

I bring my eyes back to his now-darkened eyes. A predator ready to attack his prey. Moments feel like eternity, standing in front of his naked body, aching for his touch. One hand makes its way up to caress my cheek, holding my gaze. His eyes drift down to my lips, and in a swift moment, they collide with his. I grip the back of his neck, pulling him in closer as I open my mouth slightly to welcome his tongue as it grazes mine. His hands grip my hips again, pulling me into him. I can feel his length on my waist, growing harder with every swift movement of our tongues together. He grips my ass in both hands, pulling me up to my tip toes. My back collides with the shower wall as he pushes up against me harder, knocking over a few stray bottles. We don't even acknowledge the crash that sounds when they hit the floor. Our bodies continue to intertwine with each other. After a moment of being pinned against the wall, he leans down slightly to lift me, allowing me to wrap my legs around his waist. Our kiss deepens.

He stretches back and shuts off the water before it runs cold. He grips my hips and carries me out of the shower, gently setting me on the bathroom counter. Our tongues continue to invade each other's mouths as he reaches up and unhooks my bra, my breasts springing free. I rip the bra off my arms, sending it flying across the room. I hook my legs around him, pulling him closer until I can feel every throbbing inch of him. The wild, burning sensations grow stronger deep inside me as his fingers dig into my hips, pulling me into him. Even with my jeans still on, I can feel him push up against my sensitive spot. A small moan escapes past my lips, vibrating his mouth. His lips travel down my jaw, then down my neck. I throw my head back as his kisses reach my breast. My erect nipple is held between his front teeth as he gives them a light tug. A shock wave shoots through my body, and another moan escapes. A growl comes from him as he brings his lips back to mine, sweeping me up into his arms again and carrying me into the bedroom. He drops me onto the bed, soaking the sheets. His hands travel down to the waistband of my pants. He hesitates and pulls away from me. Before he could say anything, I run my hand through his black, wet hair, pulling him back to me.

I don't want him to go through the process of asking me if I'm sure or not. I don't want him to talk. I want him to touch me, to kiss me. Almost losing him tonight nearly broke me. Instead of just informing a chief and having someone with the right equipment go in and get him, I risked my own life. I disobeyed orders to save him. I knew the longer I waited, the bigger the chance of him being dead was. It made me realize that I would have rather died beside him than stand back and only hope.

His hand continues down to my pants, unbuttoning them painfully show, sliding his hand along my skin down to the pulsing bundle of nerves craving touch. His fingers graze my clit, and I arch my back at the touch. He runs his finger back and forth, up and down. As his hand works, his lips suckle at my neck against my raging pulse. The longer his fingers work, the closer to the edge I get, but he pulls away. Sitting up, he hooks his now wet fingers on the waistband of my pants and pulls them down past my thighs, my knees, my ankles, then completely off, taking my underwear along with it, completely exposing me on the soaked sheets. He crawls back to me, spreading my legs open for him. Our lips collide again, more hungry than before. His tip swirls around my entrance, and I arch my back, begging for more just before he slowly slides himself in barely an inch with ease. He hesitates.

"Are you sure?" He whispers in my ear.

I nod.

With that approval, he thrusts the rest of the way in, filling me more than I anticipated. I gasp as he pulls out and then pushes back into me. He begins a rhythmic motion, and I claw into his back. A soft groan comes from deep within him, and he thrusts harder.

In, out. In, out.

The feeling of him is like nothing I imagined. Those accidental fantasies in the shower were nothing compared to this.

He slides one hand under my lower back, pulling me up slightly and elevating my hips as he thrusts in and out of me.

A loud moan escapes me this time as pleasure rushes through my body. His lips travel up and down my neck, forcing out more and more moans and soft squeaks from me.

Tension begins to build inside me. Both our panting starts to quicken when he gives one last, hard thrush, pushing as deep into me as he can. A loud growl announcing his climax. And with that, pleasure explodes inside me, and a loud moan joins his.

He remains inside me as I pulse around him, panting, completely and utterly satisfied.

CHAPTER

25

S tanding in the living room, I look around at the birthday decorations plastered on the walls. Laughing children run by me, smacking each other with balloons.

"Careful, kids!" My mom shouts out, lifting a plate of cheese and crackers out of the way of the kid's heads. She passes me wearing a white sundress, her platinum blonde hair in loose curls falling down her shoulders, her skin golden tan with a light, highlighting glitter on her collar bone. She doesn't notice me. No one notices me standing by the couch.

"Mom!" A young boy's voice calls out from the stairs.

I see a teenage boy dressed in blue jeans, a Blink 182 t-shirt, and Converse sneakers. "Where's my skateboard?"

"In the garage, honey! Where I told you to put it."

Dylan.

Dylan's dark hair shines in the sunlight coming in through the windows.

After Dylan vanishes into the garage, a little girl runs through the backyard's sliding glass door.

"Can we have cake now?!" She shouts.

She has long, nearly black hair, a white dress with pink flowers, pink rubber sandals, and a birthday hat strapped to her head. She bounces up and down at the kitchen island as my mom sets out more snacks. "And ice cream?! " she adds.

It's me. The young girl is me. It's my 8th birthday party. I recognize my mother's white dress and the decorations.

My mom looks down at young me with a big smile.

"Who said you get cake and ice cream?" She teases.

"Mom!" Young me shouts.

"Of course, the birthday princess gets cake and ice cream!" A deep voice comes from behind me. I flinch at the tone.

My Father walks past me again, not noticing me standing in the doorway, shocked. I look back to see young me jumping with joy just before my father reaches down and lifts young me onto his hip, a big smile on his face. He leans over and gives my mother a light kiss. She looks at him with so much love on her face—a look I haven't seen since my father passed away.

What is this? Why can't anyone see me?

My father ambushes young me with kisses. I remember the feeling of his scruff rubbing on my young, soft skin. Young me giggles at the feeling.

"Alright, everyone!" my father shouts out. "The birthday girl wants her cake! Everyone in the dining room!"

My father walks over and sets young me down in a chair at the head of the table. My mother meets us with a rainbow cake covered in sprinkles and lit birthday candles- the same big smile still plastered on her face. She sets the cake down in front of the past me, bouncing up and down. She joins my father as he wraps his arm around her waist, giving her a gentle kiss on her cheek.

I grew up hoping for love like my parents. Hoping I would find a man that would love and treat me the way my father loved my mother. I don't think I ever saw my mother sad when she was around my father, and I never saw my father upset around her. They always had smiles on their faces and teased and giggled like they were still a new couple in high school. Young me looks up to my loving parents as the kids with the balloon run past the table, the movements blowing the candles out. My young face drops, and I look back to my father, eyes widening.

"Daddy! My candles!" She cries out.

"What about them?" He asks calmly.

I watch confused like he didn't just see what happened. He waves a hand towards the candles.

"They're just fine."

The candles on the cake ignite again with a wave of his hand before my young eyes can make their way back.

Holy shit.

I continued watching as young me jumped for joy, seeing the candles still lit. My mother didn't even see what happened. None of the kids saw. That's where my powers came from. The fire dancer was right about it being genetic. As everyone begins to sing, a dark fog flows around me. I flinch, frantically looking around at the dark cloud covering me. When it clears, I'm back in the living room. But this time, it's dark. Tyler sits in the recliner, slumped over, playing his gameboy. The dim light shone on his young face. Candles are lit throughout the house. My mother sits on the couch with a heavy blanket wrapped around her while young me clings to her body for warmth.

The power is out.

I look out the window to see heavy snow covering every surface outside.

I remember this winter storm. It was the snow we had gotten the most since I was alive. It took out power lines, and we sat in the dark all night. It wasn't bad until about hour 8 when all the heat in the house had cooled. We all crammed in the living room, trying to stay warm while we waited for my dad to get home from work. It was taking him longer than usual because of the snow.

Dylan comes into the living room with more blankets.

The front door swings open just then, letting in cold wind and snow. We all cringe at the cold air while my dad, still in his navy blue uniform, forces the door shut again.

He grunts and shivers off the ice.

"Daddy!" Young me shouts from my mother's embrace.

"No fire?" He asks as he drops his overnight bag by the door.

"I couldn't get it lit. The lighters are dead." My mother says between hello kisses.

He nods and walks over to the fireplace.

I join him, watching him fumble around with firewood.

"Dylan?" He asks out loud.

"Yeah, Dad?" Dylan responds, putting an extra blanket around young me and tucking her in tight.

"Do me a favor, go in the camping gear in the garage, and get the lanterns. Get some batteries out of the kitchen drawer and light them so we can have some light. Tyler, go into the hall closet and grab some board games. That battery isn't going to last all day."

Tyler sighs but obeys, and both boys leave the room.

I watch them leave momentarily before returning my attention to my father at the fireplace. He sets up some firewood and hovers his hands over the logs. His fingertips glow as flames ignite around the wood. They do the same seductive dance.

"How was work, hon?" My mother asks as the flames begin to illuminate the room.

"Busy." He responds, standing up to join us on the couch.

He grunts as he plops down, wrapping his arm around my mother. She leans her head down on his shoulder. The younger version of myself gets up and crawls over to my father's lap, wrapping her arms around him.

I never missed a chance to cuddle with my dad, even if he smelled like soot and old, sick people.

He wraps a heavy blanket around young me, pulling her closer.

Dylan soon returns with some lanterns.

"We haven't been able to cook anything today," my mother whispers to my father. "The kids have been having cereal and snacks. I don't know what we're going to do for dinner."

My father nods as he thinks for a moment.

"The barbecue is in the backyard. I can fire it up." He leans down to young me, face buried in his chest. "How's barbecue chicken and corn sound tonight?"

Young me wiggles and nods at him. He passes her back to my mother and gets up from the couch.

"Alright, boys. Let's get the barbecue out and fired up."

Even after a 24-hour shift of nonstop work, he still takes the time to care for his family. He spent the rest of that day warming up the house, clearing snow off the roof, and cutting down branches that were close to falling. He worked till late that night before I fell asleep on his lap by the fire. I never appreciated it as much as I do now.

When even exhausted, his family was his priority.

I flinch awake just as thunder cracks outside. Rain hits the bedroom window as the wind blows. I sit up, looking to my left. Colson is still peacefully sleeping beside me, the sheets covering just above his waist. His breathing is quiet, slow, and calm. I pull my knees up to my chest and wrap my arms around them as I process everything.

I never noticed my dad use his powers growing up. I wish he were still around to teach me how to use mine.

I pull my knees closer as a single tear goes down my cheek. Just as I go to whip it away, a hand caresses my back.

"You okay?" Colson's sleepy voice says.

I nod. "Just a dream."

"A bad one?" He asks.

I shake my head. "My dad was in it."

He lets out a soft hum before pulling me closer to him. I let my body fall beside him, curling up into his arms. He takes a deep breath, letting it out slowly as he rubs my back. I lay against his bare chest, listening to his heartbeat slow back down and feeling the rise and fall of his chest. I breathe in his scent, allowing myself to drift back to sleep.

CHAPTER

26

I open my eyes just long enough to squint them again from the bright sun coming in from the bedroom window. The smell of fresh rain and damp earth fills the room. A cool breeze caresses my face. Colson must have cracked the window open when he got up this morning.

I shift in the sheets, feeling the soft fabric across my still-naked body. My body protests at any moment. Practically yelling at me.

Stop moving and rest.

My arms are weak from exerting my powers to save us in the fire. I ignore my body's pleas to rest and crawl out of the comfort of Colson's bed. Goose bumps cover my skin as the cool, post-storm air kisses parts of my body that are used to being covered. I dig through the clothes hung up neatly on hangers and grab the first oversized t-shirt I can find. An old, overworn Nirvana t-shirt covers just below my ass, enough to get me by.

I follow the clinking of dishes coming from the kitchen, soon hearing Colson's deep mumbling. I enter the kitchen to find him standing at the stove in nothing but dark grey sweatpants hanging low on his waist. He tilts his head, holding his phone to his ear with his shoulders, the muscles tense along his back. He turns his head just enough to notice me coming in. His face is serious until our eyes lock, and then his smile grows so big that it makes his eyes squint, a toothpick between his stunning white teeth. He nods once, then gestures to the chair at the island, where an empty plate sits on a place mat with a glass and a jug of orange juice, some fresh fruit, butter, and syrup.

"Right." He huffs into his phone. "They have any idea who?"

His voice is stern and serious.

"And the cameras?" He pauses. "Right. Keep me filled in if you find anything. We'll be in later to fill out a report."

He drops his phone and hits the end button without saying goodbye. He lifts the pan and turns to come beside me to plop fresh blueberry pancakes on the plate in front.

"Coffee is almost ready." He says softly before planting a light kiss on my head. I look up to him and watch him make his way back to the stove, the muscles in his back flexing with every movement.

"Who was that?" I ask, smothering the pancakes in butter.

"That was Paulson. He says they think the fire last night was arson."

I glance back at him, cutting into the food before me.

"Arson? Really?"

He turns around with a fresh cup of coffee, sets it down for me, and then heads to the fridge to grab the bottle of creamer.

"They found some gas tanks near where they think the fire started. They're sending them to a neighboring county to get them tested for prints while our station is down."

"What about the security cameras?"

"Too damaged in the fire. We lost a lot last night. Luckily, most of our stuff had been downloaded onto hard drives that survived. But any physical evidence. They're going to go through and see what is damaged and what is salvageable."

I don't remember how destructive the fire was when we got out of it since I was more focused on not blacking out. We left before they had it under control, too. Both Colson and Cap were pissed and just wanted me out of the way, so I didn't go running back in there.

"Do you think it was Trevor?" I ask before even thinking.

Colson grabs his food and coffee and joins me.

"It's hard to say. It could have been anyone. Cops make a lot of enemies."

He's not wrong. Police are definitely some of the least loved first responders.

"They want us to make a statement."

I take a sip of coffee before responding. "Why?"

"Just to see if we saw anything."

"I got there after the fire had already taken over, though."

"But you were inside it with me. So I guess that counts for something."

I huff a breath and return to my coffee.

I sit for a moment, rethinking the events of last night. I had such tunnel vision when it came to running in that building. All I was concerned about was getting in and getting Colson out. If I was working, I would have been more likely to look around. We were trained to keep our eyes peeled when on site for safety reasons and to help the investigators in case it was an arson. But all my training went out the window at that moment.

"Can I ask you something?" Colson's voice breaks the silence.

"Mhm," I hum.

"What was your dream about last night? It seemed like it affected you a lot."

I set my cup down without fully letting go of it.

"It wasn't so much of a dream as a memory."

"What do you mean?"

I don't dare look at the confusion on his face.

"Back when I was 8, my parents had a birthday party for me. When I was getting ready to blow out my candles, some kids ran by and made them go out before I had the chance. I just remember looking at my dad, who said they were fine, and when I looked back, they were still lit. I didn't think anything of it then, but I saw it from a different perspective last night. It was him that re-lit them while I wasn't looking."

Colson only studies my face as I continue.

"Then, when I was younger, we had that big snowstorm come through that knocked out power for a few days."

"I remember that." He says.

"My mom couldn't get any lighters in the house to work, so she couldn't get the fire lit. But when my dad came home, all he did was wave his hand over the fireplace, and it lit. But he hid it from all of us."

"So you got your powers from him?"

I nod. "I think so."

"Are you wanting to get yourself killed?!" Cap screams at me.

I sit in front of his desk, elbows resting on my knees, hands clasped together, and eyes straight down, accepting the scolding.

"You deliberately disobeyed my orders to stay back. You ran into that building with no PPE or any equipment. You risked the lives of you and all your fellow firefighters. What were you thinking?"

My eyes drift up to his.

"I asked for help."

"From who?!" He shouts. "Not from me! Not from Fitz. Not from anyone on our crew."

"It was the nearest firefighter that was there."

"The one you confronted."

I nod. "I told him Colson was still in there. He only brushed it off. I couldn't risk the time it took to inform anyone else and get a team together. So I took a chance and ran in."

He sighs, rubbing the bridge of his nose.

"You almost got yourself killed." He says softly.

"I know." I nearly whisper, dropping my head down again.

After being scolded for what felt like forever, I leave the office to find Colson sipping a coffee as he looks at his phone. I walk over and lean against the counter next to him.

Our eyes meet, but we say nothing, the apparent look on my face that I just got scolded.

We spent the rest of the day talking about the fire with investigators and other detectives, repeating the same thing over and over like a broken record. By the time we finally got back to the house, we both were so mentally exhausted that we fell asleep on the couch as a movie played. The following day was the typical breakfast and coffee at the kitchen island. Just as breakfast was done, my brother Dylan called me asking if he could visit. Colson said of course.

The rain let up just as Dylan's truck pulled into the driveway. I make my way off the front porch when Claire comes barreling out of the truck towards me. She leaps into my arms with laughter as I try to keep us from falling over.

"It hasn't been that long since I saw you guys last." I laugh.

"I know!" She laughs back. "I just missed my sis-in-law!"

She pushes me arms-length away and looks me over. Her eyes hesitate on my knee brace, which is still holding me together.

"It'll be on a little longer. Almost out of it." I smile, reading her mind.

Her eyes meet mine just as the sun peaks around a cloud. Her attention shoots behind me. I follow her glance to see Colson stepping through the door.

"Is that him?" She mouths the words.

I chuckle. "Claire, this is Colson."

Colson smiles. "So nice to meet you! I've heard a lot of good things."

Claire looks back at me, eyes wide, and her mouth forms the words "Oh my God " before patting me on the shoulder and walking over to shake Colson's Hand.

"Hey, Sis." Dylan's voice drags my attention away.

"Hey, Bro," I say as I wrap my arms around him.

"How's the leg?"

I glance down at my brace and then back to him.

"Better. I was just telling Claire that I'll be out of the brace soon."

"That means back to work?"

I nod. "Light duty. I won't be able to run into burning buildings, but I can at least help on medical calls. It'll be nice to be back to work, though. Been locked up in the house too long."

Dylan's eyes drift over the house. "At least it's a nice house."

I let out a light laugh and watch Claire and Colson casually converse. Claire was as animated as ever.

"Hey," my attention goes back to Dylan. Standing tall over me, looking so much like our father. "I brought you something." He points to the bed of his truck.

He pulls the tarp away, exposing my matte black 2018 Yamaha R6. I gasp at the sight of it. Dylan had it stored in his garage since I moved into my apartment. I chose to leave it behind when I moved.

"I washed it for you. Now it can get the hell out of my garage and be ridden again like it's supposed to."

He dropped the tailgate down, pulling a box closer. Inside is all my riding gear and helmet.

"Hey, Colson! You mind giving me a hand with this?" Dylan shouts over my shoulder.

Colson nods before patting Claire's shoulder and jogging over. I step back and rejoin Claire to watch the guys unload the bike.

"He's something." She chuckles to me.

"He is."

CHAPTER

27

B y the time Dylan and Claire left, it was late. Colson had received a call and had to go handle some business, so he left me alone at the house while they were here, figuring my big brother would be enough protection in case something was to happen.

I was in the kitchen making a cup of tea when I heard the front door open and close. I froze for a moment, listening to make sure it was Colson coming home. An odd jingling noise rang out.

Keys? Maybe?

Doesn't sound like his keys. My body freezes again as the sound continues. A light thump, then a ticking noise comes rushing down the hallway. Just as I reach for a knife on the counter, a pure black German shepherd comes rushing into the room, tail wagging as he sees me. The dog comes rushing up to me, ears pinned back, tail wagging so powerfully it whacks every surface in its way.

"Well, hello there," I say in a high-pitched voice, releasing the knife in my hand and replacing it with head scratches. The dog loses all control of his body as I scratch and pat his sides.

I laugh as I watch him, so full of excitement, like he's been waiting his whole life to meet me.

"That's Kujo." Colson's voice sounds from the doorway.

I look up to see him leaning against the archway, arms crossed.

"You went and got a dog?"

He chuckles. "Something like that." He walks over to join us, Kujo now wagging his tail at him. "He's a K9 from the department. He was in training but was deemed 'too friendly' to be part of the department. He would do the bite work fine but release the sleeve and begin cuddling with the decoy."

I look down at Kujo just as his tongue slaps me across the face.

"His protection instincts are still there. He will protect you when I'm not around."

I meet Colson's dark brown eyes looking down at me.

"They just let you take him?"

Kujo nearly knocks me over, trying to lean against me.

"It took some convincing. He was going to go to a kill shelter if I didn't." He leans down and scratches Kujo behind the ears. Pure pleasure is all over Kujo's face. "He's too good of a boy to go to that hell hole."

"You picked him up just to protect me?"

A smirk grows on his face. "And to keep you company."

I huff a laugh. I can't be mad while Kujo is snuggled up to me. His appearance is intimidating, but his friendly demeanor overpowers his looks.

That night, Kujo stayed close to my side, not letting me out of his sight for a second. He slept at my feet all night. Colson tried to protest him sleeping in the bed with us, but Kujo didn't budge. He took his role as my personal bodyguard very seriously. I didn't mind having a shadow now—especially one as cute as him. In the morning, I woke up with Kujo right at my side, tail wagging as I rolled out of bed.

Colson walks out of the bathroom, a towel around his waist. I twist around to look at him over my shoulder, and my eyes immediately migrate to places lower. The perfect, chiseled abs with a perfect V trailing under the towel. The tiny bit of chest hair right between his toned pecks and another patch right in the middle of the V line. Tattoos shimmer, still damp from his morning shower.

God damn, he's like a Greek god.

He brushes his wet, black hair back out of his face and gives me a smirk.

"Good morning, love." He purrs.

His voice rattles me deep inside. I have already had him, but I still seem to get butterflies from his voice alone. I smile back at him, pushing the little chunk of hair that has grown long enough to cover my face.

He struts over and crawls across the bed until he's nose to nose with me, my cheeks heating at the proximity. His minty breath overwhelms my senses. His soft lips graze mine, depriving me of the full touch. Just before our kiss could become just that, a hurricane of black fur barrels between us, bombarding us with kisses and uncontrollable body movements. Colson sits back, allowing Kujo to barrel into his lap and roll over onto his back, legs kicking in excitement.

"I have to go into town to do a few things," Colson says softly. "Would you two like to come?"

The question was directed more toward the dog than me. Kujo wiggles in response.

"I think he could use a walk around the city." I laugh.

Colson drops me off near my favorite coffee shop, trusting Kujo to protect me every step of the way. So far, he is doing a pretty good job. The few people walking down the sidewalk clear the way for us, avoiding eye contact with the near Werewolf of a dog by my side. No one protests as I walk him into the coffee shop, get my coffee and continue down the street on our walk. After a few blocks, Kujo stops dead in his tracks, the feathers on his back stand straight up. He lets out a rumbling growl ahead of us, his white teeth shining bright against his black coat. I look down at him and then up ahead, where something bothers him. The sidewalk is clear, but I recognize where we are. The alleyway where I was attacked is just ahead. But I can't see anything that would trigger a response like the one Kujo has. I try to continue forward, but Kujo's growling grows louder. I can see how he would be a good protection dog. Not only does he look terrifying when he's not wagging his tail uncontrollably, but his growl is enough to rumble the city.

I pull Kujo along as we head down the alley to cut through to the rest of the shops. He reluctantly comes along with me, sticking close to my left side.

"Codi." A voice calls out from behind me.

I jump, and Kujo lunges, barking and growling like a rabid animal. I hold him back as much as I can.

"Trevor?" I ask.

Trevor stands before me in a black hoodie, dirty jeans, and a baseball cap.

"You got a dog?" he asks.

I look down at Kujo, who is still growling with hackles raised high.

"He was a gift."

Not a lie. Colson did get him for me.

"From your new boyfriend?"

My head twitches from the word, and my face drops.

"Wha..What do you mean?"

"He's a cop, isn't he?"

Detective. But, whatever.

I don't argue the technicalities in hopes that he's only trying to get information from me.

"What are you talking about, Trevor?"

"I sent you packages." He ignores my questions.

"I know," I whisper.

He steps closer to me, and Kujo releases another warning growl that halts him.

"You're living with him, aren't you?"

I say nothing.

"Your landlord said you haven't been home in weeks. But cops have been in and out of the unit with boxes and bags of things."

Colson sent officers to my apartment when I needed a few things. I stared at Trevor, waiting for him to get to his point. Kujo's growl vibrated my leg. I slowly reached for my back pocket, where my phone sat snugly. If I could just call Colson, he would overhear the conversation and send officers my way.

"Don't do that." Trevor snaps, pulling a gun out of his hoodie pocket.

Kujo's growl grows, and he flinches towards Trevor.

"You're not going to call him. He's not going to take me."

I look down at the gun, only pointing to the ground.

"Trevor," I say softly. "What did you do?"

His eyes meet mine.

"Do you love him?" He asks, avoiding the question again.

I bite my lip at the question.

"Trevor," I whisper.

"Do you LOVE HIM!" He ends the question with a yell, and I flinch but say nothing.

"He was supposed to die the other night."

My eyes widen. "It was you?"

"But, you went in after him."

"You were there?"

"You almost died."

I'm getting frustrated with how many times he avoids my questions.

"How did you get out alive?" He asks, his head tilted to the side. His eyes look entirely different from when we were in love. It's almost like he's possessed. His light blue eyes are nearly gray now. Dead inside.

"What did you do, Trevor." My voice came out rougher, like Kujo's growl.

My phone begins to ring in my back pocket. Trevor's brow rises, nearly telling me not to even think about answering it. It goes to voicemail, then begins ringing again. I don't take my eyes off Trevor and his gun.

"I loved you." He whispers. "All I ask is for another chance."

"Trevor, this isn't the way to convince me to give you another chance. Killing people, burning buildings down, threatening me."

"Im. Not. Threatening."

"you have a gun," I say. My eyes darted to the gun in his hand.

"Please." He says softly.

"You're doing the opposite of convincing me to give you another chance. You've gone too far. Those girls didn't deserve what you did to them."

His blank stare gives me the confirmation I was looking for. He doesn't deny that he killed those girls or that he was behind the arson that nearly killed Colson.

Before he could say anything, the revving of a truck engine came from behind me.

Trevor takes off running in the opposite direction, and Kujo lunges, wanting to chase him, but I hold him back. Nothing is stopping Trevor from shooting him.

"Get in the truck!" Colson's voice calls out.

I didn't even notice he got out of the truck until he grabbed the leash out of my hand and placed his hand on my lower back, ushering me to the already open passenger side door. I get in the truck just before Colson slams the door.

"Stay in the truck." He orders after putting Kujo in the back seat. He jogs around the corner, hitting a button on his phone and putting it to his ear.

CHAPTER

28

I sit on the edge of Colson's truck, petting behind Kudos ears, watching Colson talking to other officers. He nods his head and turns to walk back to me.

"So?" I ask.

He seems frustrated, but I can't tell if he's mad at me or the situation.

"They lost him."

I take a deep breath just as Kujo leans against me, nearly pushing me off the edge. Colson stares at Kujo.

"What did he say to you?" He asks.

"Not really anything. Just that he wished I would give him another chance."

"Did he admit to anything?"

I shake my head. "No. But, he also didn't deny anything."

Colson's dark eyes meet mine, mixed with annoyance and relief.

"Okay." He huffs, patting my leg. "Let's get you two home. I have a few more things I have to do now. I'll have an officer outside the house in case I'm out late."

I nod.

Each step I take ripples the thin layer of water surrounding me. Nothing but darkness reflects off the glass-like layer. I lift my hand up and summon flames to illuminate my surroundings. It doesn't do much of anything with the void surrounding me. I notice a layer of smoke flowing towards me. It engulfs the area.

Codi.

a voice calls out from the darkness. I whip around in the direction it came from to see nothing but black smoke.

Codi.

another voice, this time different. I spin on my heel again, only to be met with more smoke.

"Hello?" *I call out.*

"look what you did." *The voice echoes.*

I keep spinning in hopes of seeing where the voice is coming from, but I am only met with smoke. A faint orange glow ignites in the smoke.

"What have you done?"

The voice sounds like Colson, but I can't find it.

"What?" *I call out, but it sounds like I'm yelling in water. Muffled.*

"What have you done?" *The voice calls again. This time, it sounds like Cap.*

"Cap?!" *I call out.*

"What have you done?" *Now, my father's voice.*

"Dad?!"

What have you done? What have you done? What have you done?

The voices begin to chant.

What have you done? What have you done? What have you done?

Panic builds in my gut.

What have you done? What have you done? What have you done?

The smoke surrounding me ignites into flames, shooting far taller than I can see.

What have you done? What have you done? What have you done?

"No!" I shout. "I didn't mean to!"

What have you done?!

"I swear! I didn't mean to!"

WHAT HAVE YOU DONE?!

The voices chant louder and louder, echoing around me.

"NO!" I scream.

"Codi..." *A whisper.*

I jolt awake, my heart racing. The house is calm and quiet, with only the TV screen illuminating the living room.

Are you still watching?

Obviously, not Netflix. But thanks.

Kujo sleeps soundly on my legs, a quiet snore coming from him with every breath. His eyes jolt open when the lock on the door clicks. He jumps up with just one rumbling bark and jogs off to investigate. The sound of his tail hitting the walls tells me Colson is home. I wipe my face, feeling a bead of sweat on my brow. I look over my shoulder to watch Colson walk in, holding a bag of things from the 24-hour convenience store down the road.

"Did I wake you?" He asks softly.

"No. I just woke up not long before you came in."

I look at my phone to see it's past 2 am.

"Working late?" I ask.

He nods. "I wanted to be home hours ago."

I reach to turn off the TV, hearing Colson dig around in the kitchen drawers before joining me on the couch. He falls next to me with a grunt and then reaches into the plastic bag. He lifts a pint of Ben and Jerry's ice cream and smiles.

"I remember you said Cherry Garcia was your favorite."

I could not resist the smile that grew on my face. I squeezed and grabbed the ice cream from his hands. We sat in silence for a moment, enjoying our ice cream.

"No sign of Trevor?"

He shakes his head. "It's like he vanished. I got officers searching the whole city."

"What flavor did you get?" I ask, hoping to change the subject.

He holds up the container. "Strawberry Cheesecake."

"Can I try some?"

His eyes dart to mine, and he smirks. "Sure."

I bring my spoon up, but he smacks it away.

"Let me, " he says, using his spoon to scoop a bit out and holding it out for me.

I shyly look up to him and smile. I open my mouth, feeling the cold steel of the spoon glide across my tongue. I wrap my lips around it, severing the creamy ice cream with chunks of gram crackers and strawberries.

"Good?" He asks, not taking his eyes off my lips.

I nod.

He nods his head once at mine. I scoop him some and hold it out for him. Before he could get his lips around it, I quickly jerked it over to smear it all over his cheek. His mouth drops open in shock and I can't help my childish giggle.

"Ops." I chuckle.

"That's it." He says, grabbing the ice cream from my hands and slamming it on the table. He lunges for me, and I squeal. He pins me down under him and begins to wipe the cream from his face onto mine. Laughter erupts from both of us.

"How do you like it now?" He laughs.

Our eyes lock. I raise my hand and graze his sharp jawline, covered in a day-old shadow. Each rough hair pricks my fingertips as I glide across them. I pull his face closer and run my tongue across where the melted ice cream runs down his cheek.

I watch his eyes darken a few shades before he leans in and slams his lips to mine. I open my mouth slightly to welcome him. My hands drift up and down his body, digging my nails into his back. A groan comes from deep inside him when I do. His hips press against me, and I swear I can feel every inch of him, even through the jeans. My body aches for him even more.

His hands explore my body, gliding up under my shirt, only for him to discover I'm not wearing a bra. He cups my breast in his hand and gently squeezes. A moan escapes my lips, vibrating against his. His hands, still cold from the ice cream, travel down my skin painfully slow until they reach the waistband of my sweatpants. I arch my hips against him more, begging for him to continue.

"Do you want more?" He growls.

I nod almost franticly. Something primal overcomes his eyes. Instead of scaring me, it awakens the goddess in me. Our lips collide again, tongues fighting each other for more space. His fingers trail down, down, down until his cold finger grazes my clit. I gasp at the sudden coldness in such a sensitive spot.

"Beg for it." He growls again.

"Please," I beg, obeying his command.

He plunges a finger inside me, the coldness sending a shock wave inside me. I gasp against his lips and dig my nails into his back. A smirk grows on his lips, a dominant male taking pride in his work. He slides another painfully cold finger inside, and my back arches, grinding myself against him.

"Good girl." He purrs.

His kisses trail across my face, lining my jaw, then down my neck. With each suckling kiss along my neck, the wetness between my legs grows. His fingers rip out of me, then rip the shirt off of my body, exposing my erect nipples, shocked from the sudden cold. His mouth quickly wraps around my breast, gently taking my nipple between his teeth. I arch against him, throwing my head back into the throw pillow. He continues his kissing down my abdomen until he reaches my waist. His fingers hook along the waistband and slowly pull down. I arch my hips, allowing the sweatpants to slide off with ease.

He sits up momentarily, long enough to rip off his shirt before returning to what he was doing. His tongue grazed the point where my legs met the rest of my body, and I couldn't help but let a moan break free. He travels over to my center and lightly kisses my clit. I arch into him.

"So wet for me."

His voice vibrates in this sensitive area, and I can't seem to catch my breath now. His mouth latches around me, gently suckling and licking up and down. I reach back and grip the pillow my head now rests on, my nails nearly ripping into the fabric with every pass of his tongue. He throws my legs over his shoulders and grips my hips, pulling me closer to him as he devours me. A loud moan echoes through the house, and I grow closer to climax. He lifts his gaze, my arousal plastered across his face like a wild predator. He climbs back up to me, and his lips crash into mine. I run my fingers into his hair, never wanting to let him go—the taste of me all over his mouth. I reach down and franticly undo his belt. He pulls his pants down the rest of the way, allowing himself to spring free, then plunges himself into me. I gasp at the fullness of him. He digs his fingers into my hip and pulses in a euphoric rhythm.

Our moans harmonize, and I feel so close to completion.

No, not yet.

"Sit back," I say, pulling away from him.

he cocks his head at me but obeys, gently pulling out of me. He sits back on the couch as I climb on and startle him.

"My turn." I purr into his ear before seating myself on him.

He lets out a shaky breath as my body grips around him. I take his face in my hands as I begin riding him, grinding against him. His lips travel from mine down my neck. His hands travel up my body, clawing at my back. Only the sound of our bodies colliding, our moans, and heavy breathing echo down the halls, drowning out the rain that is beginning to come down outside. I feel a tightness deep inside me when he stops me. He pushes me off of him and back onto the couch. Confused, I watch him bring himself to his knees on the couch beside me.

"Turn around." His voice was more profound than usual. Demanding.

I listen and turn away from him. He grabs my hips, pulling me to him. The fullness returns as he plunges in deep, hitting that perfect spot. I scream out a moan as he rhythmically hits that spot over and over. I'm jerked upright by his hand wrapped around my throat, pulling my back against him as he continues his rhythm. He squeezes just hard enough to cut off blood flow but not air. My moan vibrates against his hand. His lips graze my ear, nibbling softly.

"You're mine." He whispers.

With those words, I erupt in pleasure, letting a scream escape and throwing my head back onto his shoulder. He plunges against that spot one last time before pushing as deep as possible and letting out a growl into my ear as he finishes inside me.

CHAPTER

29

My phone vibrates next to me on the nightstand. I squint at the sudden light.

Unknown
Attachment: 1 Photo

I open the photo to see a young girl tied to a chair, covered in blood, wearing nothing but an old t-shirt. Just as I go to wake Colson, another message comes through.

Unknown
Don't tell him about us, baby.
If you do, she dies.
Meet me.

A second later, a location is sent through. I glance at Colson, still sleeping soundly, mouth slightly open.

Fuck.

I slowly crawl out of the bed, find some clothes, and head for the door. Kujo perks his head up.

"Kujo, Stay," I whisper to him, holding a hand up.

He cocks his head but obeys. I manage to put on my clothes and make my way to the garage door without making much noise. I shut the door and turn to the box of riding gear sitting next to my bike. My riding jacket fits more snugly than the last time I put it on, but I manage. I roll open the garage door, trying my best not to make any noise. I open it just enough to be able to roll the bike under. I push the bike down the driveway and onto the road, far enough away that I shouldn't wake Colson when starting it. I climb on and strap on my helmet.

Safety first.

I take a deep breath and turn the key. It starts right away. The roaring of the engine echoed through the trees. I look back one last time to the still-dark house before pulling away.

The rain has turned into a slight mist, which pelts the visor of my helmet and beads off. My jeans are soaked.

It takes about 35 minutes to get to the location that was sent to me. An old, two-story home stands just ahead as I stop by the mailbox. It doesn't look like anyone has lived here in 60 years, maybe more. I pull my helmet off, my hair falling in my face. Trevor's car sits, parked in the driveway, with the trunk wide open. I do my best to calm my nerves as I kick out the kickstand and climb off my bike. The velcro of my gloves was louder than I hoped. Just as I set them down on the bike's gas tank, I'm blinded by headlights. I throw my hand up as a truck pulls up behind me. The lights shut off, and I was still blinded. I only hear the door slam.

"What the fuck are you doing?!"

"Colson?" I call out. "How did you-"

"Kujo started freaking out when you left."

Damn dog.

I knew he was going to bite me in the ass. I just hoped more literally.

"You're not supposed to be here!"

"I kind of figured that when you snuck out."

I lick my lips and look back at the dark house.

"He has a girl in there," I whisper.

"I'll call back up then."

"No!" I grab his hand as he goes to pull out his phone. "If he sees cops here, he's going to kill her. He may have already now that you're here."

I hold his gaze for a moment, and then he nods. "What are we going to do?"

I look back at the house. "I'm going in."

"No." He growls.

"Colson." I snap. "I have to."

Anger grows on his face. I stare at the front door, trying to gain the confidence to walk in.

"Give me your gun." I hold my hand out to Colson.

"What?" He says, shocked at my assumption that he brought it with him.

"He's not going to kill me. He wants me alive. But he won't be expecting me to have a weapon with me. If something happens, I'll have a way to protect myself."

Other than fire.

He looks up at the house and then back at me, a muscle in his jaw flexing. He lifts up his jacket, exposing his gun, strapped to his side, and holds it out for me.

"Please." He pulls the gun back before I can take it. "Let me call back up."

I hold my hand out. "When I get inside, call paramedics. Tell them to stage a few blocks down. If the girl comes out before me, take her to them."

"Codi…" he pleads.

"Then you can call for backup." I interrupt. "But only, ONLY, if I get the girl out first. Okay?"

His jaw twitches again, but he nods, handing me the gun.

"Fall back," I command, tuck the gun into the back of my jeans, then start down the walkway to the front door.

If the outside of the home looked old, the inside looked like it was trapped in the past, still furnished with old-fashioned red couches and armchairs and family photos everywhere. I picked up one at the entryway table: a mother, a father, and two young boys. A flash from an old true crime documentary plays in my head. The family went on vacation and was never seen again. The grandparents never sold the house, hoping the family would come home someday. They never did. The grandparents passed away, and no one ever did anything with the house. My heart aches at the thought of the pain those grandparents must have lived with. Knowing your children and grandchildren are out there somewhere, possibly scared and in pain or dead.

A thump sounds from upstairs, taking my attention off the missing family. I start up the stairs, each step protesting at the weight with a loud groan. A thick layer of dust coats the railing and hanging photos along the wall. A rotting smell basically punches me in the face as I reach the landing. I hold back a gag. A door at the end of the hall is cracked open, with a dim light peaking through.

This way girl. It practically whispers to me. The floor continues to creek under each step until part of the floor breaks free. I feel my knee sting as I try to catch my footing and not fall through the floor.

I swear to god, if I keep falling through floors, I'm quitting my job. If I make it out of here alive, that is.

It only takes a few steps for my knee to quit hurting. I reach the door and listen. I hear panting but from only one person. I push my hand against the door, opening it with a loud, slow creek. As I peek my head in, the girl tied in a chair screams through the tape over her mouth and starts thrashing against her restraints.

"It's okay, I'm here to help," I call out, rushing to her side. I pull out my fire department knife out of my pocket and start cutting at the ropes around her wrists. Any real firefighter will carry a knife at all times. It's a lifesaver. Literally.

She breaks free, ripping the tape off her mouth and throwing herself into me. She can't be more than 21. I wrap my arms around her, raising to my feet.

"Where is he?" I ask, pushing her within arm's length of me.

She shakes her head. "I...I... I don't know."

Tears rush down her face.

"Listen to me, there is a detective outside. Go to him. He's going to take you to safety. Okay?" She nods. "Paramedics are waiting for you. He will take you to them, and they will take you to the hospital. You can trust him. His name is Colson."

She nods as she sobs again. I push her towards the door as I hear the door behind me creek open. The girl rushes down the stairs, and I hear her bust through the door and faint sobs as she runs to Colson. I hear his truck start and squeal from the driveway, heading down the road.

Thank god he did what I told him to.

"So, you got my message."

I keep my back turned to Trevor but turn my head towards him.

"Why are you doing this?"

"Why not?" His voice is getting closer. "It's the only thing that can't get taken away from me."

"But it will."

A breath grazes my right ear, and my body tenses.

"It's everything I wanted to do to you when you left me." He whispers in my ear. "I was so angry and sad. We could have had everything. But you chose a job over me. You chose *him* over me."

I can't tell if the "him" he is talking about is my Dad or Colson.

"You always talked about wanting to be just like your dad. How much of a hero he was to you. Even when he died, you wanted to be just like him."

"What happened to him was a freak accident."

"Was it?"

His words send a shock through my system. I snap my head at him, a little shocked at how close he stands to me, feeling his breath caress my face.

"What do you mean by that?"

"Think about it, baby. Someone had to have started that fire."

My eyes widen, and flashes of that night fly through my head—the fire engulfing the building. The hazardous chemical labels plastered everywhere, the explosion blowing up half the building, and the Chief knocking on our door late at night.

"No." The word escapes before I could even think.

An evil smile grows on his face as he looks me up and down. "I didn't mean for him to die." He whispers.

I jerk my head back as he tries to brush my hair out of my face.

"Oh, baby." He coos. "It was just supposed to scare you. He wasn't supposed to go back in for that worker. Even his fellow chief told him not to." He looks me up and down again, a feral look in his eyes. "I guess you're more like him than you think."

My heart is in my throat, and my fists crack as I clench them tight, rage building inside me. I look up to the old dresser across the room, where candles flicker, dancing in the darkness.

His fingers graze my neck. I rip away from him, jerking the gun out of my jeans, aiming right between his eyes.

"Baby."

"Don't call me that." I snarl. "You don't get to call me that."

"But he does." He growls.

"He didn't kill my dad." I snarl louder, the voice nearly animalistic.

"He wasn't supposed to go back in."

"You. Killed. Him."

The flames next to me grow with every word. My finger twitches, begging to pull the trigger.

"Put the gun down."

Just as he says the words, I hear sirens in the distance. My attention shoots to the window. In a flash, the gun is thrown from my hands.

Fuck!

I shouldn't have taken my eyes off him. I'm an idiot.

A sharp pain shoots through my head as I'm slammed against the dresser, a grunt escaping me as I hit the ground. Several candles fall to the floor, throwing hot wax on the old carpet.

"Why don't you ever listen?" Trevor says.

Pain erupts in my gut as he kicks me, throwing me against the drawers.

"You never LISTEN!" He screams. He reaches down, grabs me by my jacket, and lands a punch to my left eye. I slam to the ground again.

"I'm sorry, baby. I don't want to hurt you."

I scream as I jump to my feet, lunging at him. I grip around his waist, sending both of us into the wall so hard sheetrock crumbles around us. I stand straight, throwing a few good punches at his face. He catches my wrist, pushing me back. I slam into the dresser again. I was catching my breath as he took a step towards me, blood gushing from his nose. I look to my left to see the gun on the floor. His eyes follow mine. He's closer to it than I am. There's no way I'll get there first. Instead, I jet for the door, hoping to escape the house and find officers waiting to arrest him. A shot rings out behind me, sending a chunk of the door flying.

"Codi, don't!"

I shoot through the door, ignoring his plead.

A shot rings out again as I get a few steps down the fall. I stop dead in my tracks, and a sharp pain shoots through my lower abdomen. My eyes are wide. I glance down to see blood pouring from a hole in my jacket.

Mother fucker shot me.

I slowly turn back to Trevor, who joins me in the hallway. He drops the gun, tears building in his eyes.

"We can fix this, Codi."

I push my hand against the wound, blood forcing its way through my fingers.

"You shot me."

"I know! I'm sorry! I got scared!" He pleads.

"You. Shot. Me."

The gun drops to the floor.

I feel anger building in me until something snaps. The dim light in the bedroom grows blindingly bright. Trevor turns to see a dragon-like trail of fire erupting from the room, swirling in the air, then warping tightly around me. I stare at him from under my brows, eyes darkening with anger.

"You. Shot. Me. Trevor." I growl. "You are the reason I'm here."

I didn't think his eyes could get any wider.

"And you were right."

His brows push together.

"I am just like my father."

With the words, I throw my hands in the air, sending a whirlwind of fire swirling through the hallway, surrounding us. I throw one arm, sending a rope of flames wrapping around his waist, lifting him in the air. He screams from the pain of the flames biting at his skin.

The flames grow bigger until they burst through every upstairs window. The flames lift him higher until he's almost at the ceiling. I can feel the blood rushing from not only my gunshot wound but also my nose. But I don't stop.

"Feel the pain, Trevor. The pain you put so many in. The pain you put me through."

The flames wrap around his legs, burning away his jeans and nipping at the skin beneath. The smell of burning hair and flesh overpowers my senses. His screams are all I hear. In one last push of power, I send the flames up his body, engulfing his face and traveling down his throat. When the screaming stops, I push and send his lifeless, burning corpse down the hallway.

Time slows down. I look around to see the walls peeling and falling apart from the fire, the family photos lining the walls charring, and thick smoke covering the ceiling.

Through the flames, I see red and white lights grow brighter. The sirens trying hard to break through the roaring of the fire. I drop to my knees from pure exhaustion and blood loss.

Get up, Codi.

A deep voice echoes in my head as my head begins to drop. My eyes are so heavy they close, and my head slumps low.

Get up, princess. Get up!

I snap my eyes open, doing everything I can to crawl to the stairs. The old carpet of the steps is beginning to melt under the heat. I roll onto my ass and slide down the steps one by one. Each impact sends shooting pain through my whole body. The smoke is starting to choke me, and I fight for breath.

Go, princess. Keep going!

I finally hit the bottom step. Flames erupt over my head. I throw my hands up to control them, but they refuse to listen, my powers weakening. The front door is still so far.

"I can't." The words slip from my mouth as I collapse against the staircase railings.

I should have told Colson how I felt about him, told my family I loved them, and told Kujo he was the best boy.

"I'm coming, Dad," I whisper as I roll myself down to lay my head on the melted carpet.

No. Please.

My eyes grow heavy as the smoke chokes me. I have no strength left.

As I give up, the front door slams open, smoke rushing through the opening. I use what strength I have left to open my eyes slightly and look up to see four firefighters bursting through the door.

Not just any firefighters. *My* firefighters. *My* brothers.

"Here!" Austin's voice screams out over the flames sounding so far.

Two sets of arms wrap around my arms and lift me. I'm hauled off my feet.

I look through the mask of my rescuer.

"Leo," I whisper.

"I got you, sis."

Sis.

The nickname makes me smile briefly as I lay my head on his shoulder.

The cold air shocks my lungs, which are now full of smoke and what feels like fluid. I cough violently, but nothing comes up.

Cas catches up beside us, ripping his mask off.

"Medics! NOW!" He screams.

Leo jogs with me in his arms towards the ambulance, now pulling up to the scene.

"Codi!" Colson's voice echoes out as he rushes into view.

"Colson," I say softly.

Leo sets me on the gurney before ripping his equipment off.

"Go! Drive!" He shouts at the EMT in the driver's seat.

My clothes are cut away, exposing the hole in my abdomen, pouring blood. A hand grabs mine as the guys get to work. An oxygen mask is thrown on my face, bandages slapped on my wound, and the heart monitor is put on my finger—the sound of my racing heartbeat on the machine.

"Colson," I call out hoarsely.

"I'm right here." He says, running his hand through my hair.

"It was him."

He nods.

"He killed Dad."

His eyes widen, and he looks at Leo, now attempting to put an IV in my arm.

Colson says, "You got him?"

I smile and nod. "I got him."

"Good girl." He whispers, clearing the ash from my eyelashes.

"Colson?"

"Yeah?"

I squeeze his hand tighter. "I love you."

I can see tears building in his eyes as he smiles at me.

"Yeah. I love you, too."

I smile. His handsome face begins to blur, and every muscle in my body relaxes. My hand slips from his grip. The edges of my vision go black, but I'm calm as everything fades away. The last sound I hear is the machines alerting and Leo's voice calling out.

"She's coding!"

CHAPTER

30

"Thank you all so much for joining us this evening." Chief Fitz announces to the growing crowd. Silence rings out over the bays. "We are here to not only honor an extraordinary name but to remember it as well. A name that went far greater than above and beyond for this community. A name that risked everything. And even in death, the name lives on. Whether in our hearts or the blood of their family, we remember the Dovetch name."

Several heads bow at the last name, including Kujo, who sits patiently next to Colson in the front row.

"With a loss still hurting our hearts, we also have much joy to share. Tonight, we honor the Dovetch name. With the probationary period ending, we welcome our newest, full-time firefighter." He lifts a hand. "Codi Dovetch."

The crowd erupts in applause as I make my way to the stand next to the chief, a broad smile on his face. I glance down to see my mother sitting in the front row, across the aisle from Colson and Kujo, whose tail has started uncontrollably wagging, and he yips once he spots me.

"Thank you, chief." He nods and waves to the microphone, allowing me to say a few words. I look at the extensive photo of my father on the side of the stage with unlit candles beside it. "I'm proud to stand up here today. To be alive. Most of you know we had some close calls this year. But I truly feel my father was by my side, as well as everyone in this department. He was my Superman, and many others also looked up to him. I'm proud to carry on his name in the department where he lived so many years."

I glance back down to my family. Dylan and Tyler sitting with their wives, all with a smile.

"As I officially swear in, I hold my father close to my heart. I hope to make him proud. I chose to make this night more about honoring him than celebrating myself. I wouldn't be here if it weren't for him."

I step back and allow Chief to pin my official name tag to my uniform.

"I now introduce you all to firefighter Dovetch."

The crowd stands, applauding. Kujo stood, giving his howls of excitement. My eyes meet Colson as he mouths the words, "I love you."

My heart flutters, and I return the words. Just as I do, it feels like time slows down, but I stay at normal speed. Suddenly, a single candle by my father's photo comes to life. I whip my head over to watch the small flame dance around under his face. My face drops, and I slowly glide my eyes down the center aisle between the cheering crowd. A man stands beside the engine, shining from its recent wash for tonight. He stands tall with nearly black hair and scruff like he forgot to shave, ice blue eyes meet mine and send a chill down my spine, a classic "Proud dad" smile on his face. Tears build, threatening to pour down my cheeks as I stare at this man smiling back at me. My father stands in his dress uniform.

You did so well.

His voice echoes in my mind, and a sob escapes my throat. I attempt to swallow the hysterical cries working their way up.

I will be here with you when you need me most. I will always be beside you. You did it, baby girl.

His eyes drift down, and his smile grows again. I followed his gaze to see my mother, who was turned around in her seat. She swings her head back to me, pure shock on her face, eyes wide with tears about to break free. I meet her look and nod, holding back my tears with everything I have. And for the first time in years, I see her smile. A real smile. One that is so big it reaches her eyes, causing the tears to pour down her rose-colored cheeks. We both look back at the ghost of him just as he turns away. He hesitates for a moment before gently gliding his hand on the engine. The red and white lights explode with color. The other engines and medical rigs follow in a bright flashing color. I return my gaze to my father as he smiles over his shoulder.

I'm so proud of you—my princess of fire.

As he turns away, he fades into a white mist that travels out of the open bay doors and joins the stars in the clear night sky.

I took a moment before the party to sit alone with my mother and cry after what we saw—happy tears, of course.

They pulled the engines out of the bays to open a dance floor for everyone. I sway back and forth with my arms wrapped around Colson's neck. His soft lips gently kissed mine for a moment. I smile, enjoying the moment I never knew I needed. Kujo lays on his back by a growing crowd of firefighters, wives, and kids as they rub his belly, his leg kicking violently when they hit just the right spot. He's such a vicious guard dog that just can't resist his belly rubs.

"He's loving this attention," Colson says, leaning closer to me.

I chuckle. "We might not get him back after this."

Colson huffs a laugh as we watch Kujo in pure doggy heaven. "I'm going to be sad to leave him."

Colsons head whips to look at me. "What do you mean?"

I cock my head at the question. "I'm going to have to return to my apartment at some point."

"Or maybe… you don't?"

My brows push together, waiting for him to explain. "You could always just bring your stuff to my place. Or, we could get a new place. Maybe one with a yard for your dog."

I chuckle. "He's our dog, Colson."

A smile grows on his face.

"Are you sure you want that?" I ask nervously.

"I almost lost you that night. Your heart stopped for almost ten minutes. I thought you were gone. I don't ever want to feel that again. I want you with me."

I smile and hold back another sob. "Okay," I whisper.

I glance over to see my mom sitting at a table with an older man with salt and pepper hair. She laughs at something he says, and if I didn't know any better, I would almost think she was… flirting. "Who's that?" I ask Colson, nodding to them.

"Detective Long. He trained me when I started and taught me everything I know. He's a great guy." My mother glances up to meet my eyes, a huge smile and blush even more prominent with how her face turns a rosy pink. Seeing her like that, I can't help but let a smile grow. I nod at her and give her the look of "Hell yeah, girl. Get it!"

She chuckles at my expression and returns to Detective Long.

"Is it weird seeing her with someone who's not your dad?" Colson asks, bringing my attention back to him.

"Yes. But, she deserves to be happy again."

Colson's fingertips tilt my chin to meet his eyes, the heat between us growing. He leans in and gives me a soft, loving kiss.

"Wanna get out of here?" He whispers against my mouth.

My smile takes over most of my face, and I nod.

ACKNOWLEDGMENTS

Thank you for taking the time to come on the journey, which is the first installment of The Firelight Series. I hope you enjoyed this story. I had a fantastic time bringing Codi and Colson to life and can not wait to continue with more of their wild, thrilling, and sexy adventures.

Thank you to everyone who supported this story and sat on the edge of their seats, waiting for the next chapter to be finished. Without you, this series would never have come to life.

Thank you to my *Milton and Hugo Publishing* team for bringing this story to the world and making my dream come true.

ABOUT THE AUTHOR

Maty Eitner is an up-and-coming author and a volunteer firefighter, which inspired her debut, *The Princess of Fire—The Firelight series*.

If she is not in front of her laptop or with a book in hand, she spends her little free time with her loving dog, Tao, and two cats, Donut and Olive.

She enjoys dark romance and fantasy books.
A Court of Thorns and Roses inspiring her writing career.

Instagram: @MatyEitner
Facebook: facebook.com/MatyEitner